12.95
9-09

KISS AND TELL

KISS AND TELL

•

Loretta Brabant

AVALON BOOKS
NEW YORK

Published by Thomas Bouregy & Co., Inc.
160 Madison Avenue, New York, NY 10016

Library of Congress Cataloging-in-Publication Data

Brabant, Loretta.
    Kiss and tell / Loretta Brabant.
        p. cm.
    ISBN 978-0-8034-9974-4 (hardcover : acid-free paper)
    I. Title.
    PS3602.R32K57 2009
    813'.6—dc22

                                            2009012798

PRINTED IN THE UNITED STATES OF AMERICA
ON ACID-FREE PAPER
BY HADDON CRAFTSMEN, BLOOMSBURG, PENNSYLVANIA

As this is my first book, there are so many people to thank, so many people who have supported me on this journey to becoming a published writer. I most definitely couldn't have done it without the faith of my family, particularly my parents, Ivan and Juanita, and my sisters, Jacenta, Marlena and Angela. My mother-in-law, Shirley, has also been a fountain of encouragement.

My critique group, WINK, was absolutely fantastic in helping me bring this book together. Without them, it certainly wouldn't have made it this far. Thanks guys.

And finally, to my darling husband, Todd, who has always believed in me, and my two beautiful babies . . . this book's for you.

Max Deroux's Number One Hit single

"Blue Angel"

She gets me to laugh
When I just wanna cry
When I feel like a fool
She tells me why
Hmmmmm, oh yeah

She smiles like a minx
And she sees through my soul
She knows all my faults
Yet she makes me feel bold
Hmmm, oh yeah

Loretta Brabant

I can't see the future
I don't care about the past
But she'll always be my angel,
till the very last
My sweet blue angel

She knows how I feel
Cause we are just the same
She drives me forward
Yet she sees all my pain
Hmmm, oh yeah

I can't see the future
I don't care about the past
But she'll always be my angel,
till the very last
My sweet blue angel

She's as wise as a wizard
Quick as a clock
She has the guile of a babe
Yet she knows how to shock
She's my hope
She's my faith
She's my rock

I can't see the future
I don't care about the past

But she'll always be my angel,
*   till the very last*
My sweet blue angel

Silver belle
Blue angel
Wishing well
Blue angel

She'll always be my angel
Future or past
She'll always be my angel
Till the very last.

Chapter One

You know that point when you realize you've just gone too far but it's too late to turn back? Alexis hit that point about three seconds after she threw her mini grappling hook over Ceilia Deroux's three-meter-high masonry wall.

It had all seemed so easy when Sandra explained it two days ago—almost foolproof. And with all that rock climbing she did, she'd thought it would be a cinch.

But as she looked up the unyielding plane of what was about to be her latest climb, she couldn't help but feel that reality was a bit of a slap in the face. Rock climbing was very different from scaling a smooth wall with no footholds. It was also legal.

"Alex," Sandra hissed beside her. "You're not having second thoughts, are you?"

She glanced at her fellow journalist. Dressed head to

foot in black, Sandra looked as if she'd just stepped out of some bad, low-budget, ninja film. The only parts of her exposed were her eyes and lips. Not that Alexis could talk. She looked just as bad, if not worse, in a one-piece jumpsuit that zipped right up to her chin, complete with hood.

I am insane. Alexis looked down at her leather-clad hands. *There is no other explanation for this. I am insane.*

"Alexis." Sandra gripped her shoulders and shook her. "Remember why you're doing this."

Alexis's head snapped up, and her eyes locked with Sandra's. She needed that job at *Starbuzz Magazine.* She saw her sister's children in her mind's eye and knew what she had to do—what it was her duty to do. She cleared her throat.

"Sorry."

"That's better." Sandra nodded. "Now I'm going to give you a boost." She spared a quick glance over her shoulder as she spoke.

Alexis knew exactly what she was checking for: security guards.

They had a two-minute window to get her over the wall before a guard came walking around that part of the wall again. She was wasting precious time on nerves. Clenching her teeth, she grabbed the end of the rope.

"Okay, I'm ready."

"Remember"—Sandra gripped her arm—"just as we planned. I'll meet you back at your place."

"Right." Alexis' voice quavered ever so slightly. "Just as we planned."

Sandra laced her black-gloved fingers together and held them out. Alexis tugged on the rope to make sure it was secure and then put her foot into the offered hold. Sandra heaved, and Alexis shot up half a meter. She heard the rustle of leaves below as Sandra disappeared into the trees. She clutched the rope and braced her feet against the the wall, inhaling raggedly as she took stock of her position.

The rest was up to her.

Her muscles stretched taut as she hauled herself up, pulling forward inch by inch. Hands against rope, feet against wall. The climb was not a "cinch," but it was steady. In the still of the night, the squeaking and creaking of leather gloves against straining rope sounded unnaturally loud in her ears. Her heart thudded at the very thought of being caught.

It wasn't an option.

Not with the twins waiting for her at home.

A few seconds later she reached the top of the wall. Perched there, she spent a few seconds gathering the rope up and swinging it over the wall so that it hung down the other side.

She could see the mansion now, separated from her by at least a football field's worth of garden and lake. Man, it was a stately thing, three stories tall with balconies wrapping around it at every level. It was one of Australia's heritage-listed buildings, protected and maintained not only as a home but for national pride. Looking at it now, Alexis could see why it was one of Sydney's most revered buildings. White and well lit, it

was more like a palace than a house. The garden sur-
rounds were immaculate—groomed, pruned, and drip-
ping twinkling white lights. At the center of the lake, a
dish-shaped fountain bubbled, and the faint sound of
music wafted toward her on a gentle breeze. She frowned
grimly.

The ball must be well under way by now.

Suddenly the sound of boots scraping against gravel
pricked her ears, and she realized that the security guard
was approaching right on schedule. She threw her legs
over the wall and grabbed the rope to lower herself to
the ground. Descending was much easier, and she did it
in half the time. The sound of her landing was muffled
by the grass at the base of the wall.

Her heart still pounded loudly in her ears as she listened to the footsteps pass on the other side of the wall.
She pressed her back up against its hard face and dared
not move until the sound of the footsteps had faded. As
luck would have it, it was a good thing she remained
where she was, because just at that moment a helicopter
flew overhead, dousing the ground in front of her with
light. The cylindrical beam travelled over the terrain
seemingly at random. Alexis watched it pass mere inches
from her feet, and a bead of sweat trickled down from
her temple to her chin.

Insane.

Absolutely, certifiably insane.

As the helicopter moved away, she decided to do the
same.

Staying within the shadow of the trees as much as

possible, she crept across the grounds toward the lake. Twice she stepped on a twig, almost scaring herself silly as the crackling noise burst into the silence like a triggered alarm. Each time it happened, it took her at least twenty seconds to calm herself before she could move on. She was as jumpy as a kangaroo.

Finally she reached the path that weaved around the lake, and she increased her speed. Her eyes darted cautiously from left to right as she unzipped the pouch strapped to her waist and removed a paper package.

This had better work as well as it does in the movies.

Just as she finished the thought, the barking started. Loud, angry barking that came from a distance. She unwrapped the package, revealing two large steaks barely visible in the dim lighting. Then the clicking sound of paws against pebbles became audible.

Who am I kidding? This is never going to work.

She bit her lip, bracing herself for their entrance. She had to be ready. They would be upon her in a second.

As if on cue, two dark shadows appeared on her horizon. The dogs bounded toward her, barking at the top of their lungs. Then a flash of moonlight illuminated them both briefly.

What the . . . ?

For a moment Alexis was simply struck dumb. This was not what she had been expecting at all. Labradors were not normally used as guard dogs. And these two particular specimens were absolutely gorgeous, with their shiny golden coats and big brown eyes. They stopped about a meter in front of her, sat down, and looked up adoringly at the steaks in her hands. There was not an ounce of menace in their doggy smiles and wagging tails.

"I take it you want these." She held up the steaks.

Their tongues came out, and they began panting in anticipation.

Alexis was so relieved, she began to laugh, and this action seemed to break their discipline. They immediately bounded forward, barking, jumping up on her legs and pawing at her thighs.

"Okay, okay, I get it." She chuckled and threw the steaks out in front of her. The dogs immediately made a dive for them. Alexis grinned and scooted off down the path.

Max Deroux surveyed the crowded ballroom with bitter resignation. There was no doubt that his mother had outdone herself with the party preparations. The room was a glittering array of flowers, lights, and well-dressed socialites all waiting for him.

He now wished more than ever that he had just stayed in Paris for his birthday. It was going to be a hellish night that would require the fake parade of his celebrity face— the charming Max Deroux.

Jazz singer.

Megastar.

Romantic.

A year ago he'd been all those things and more. Life had seemed so full back then, overflowing with the possibilities that success gave you. But success could take away as easily as it could give. He had been reckless.

Too reckless.

And he had paid for it.

Now he simply regarded himself as the million-dollar bachelor, a hunted man. It seemed that everywhere he turned, there was an ambitious woman offering to look after him and his wealth.

Tonight, thanks to his mother, he was clearly for sale. She should thank her lucky stars that he loved her, because if anyone else had sprung this on him, he would have walked away without apology or explanation. His privacy was something he valued very much. He had so little of it these days.

Allowing the curtain to fall discreetly back into place, he turned to his mother, who was waiting patiently for his verdict. At sixty years of age, Ceilia Deroux was an attractive woman, petite and dynamic. What she lacked in stature, she made up for in personality. He loved her dearly. But sometimes, like tonight, her impetuousness could be a tad annoying.

She cast him a pleading look with sea blue eyes the exact color of his own and clasped her hands together under her chin. "You're not mad, are you?"

He frowned pensively as his gaze tore over her. Her honey blond hair was pulled back into an elegant French roll. She wore a pale blue satin gown overlaid with delicate silvery gauze, classically cut and perfectly fitted to her trim figure. There was no doubt that she wanted this for him very much. But her goodwill was so unwarranted. Worse, it was unwanted.

"Mum, you know this is exactly what I hate."

"But, darling"—Ceilia spread her hands in appeal—"these are your friends."

Were my friends.

"Stop that." His mother playfully slapped his arm.

"Stop what?"

"Scowling."

"I'm not scowling."

"Yes, you are."

He looked down at her and despite himself smiled ruefully. "Mum, I've got nothing to say to these people."

"You won't have to say anything."

"That's what I'm afraid of."

"Nonsense," his mother admonished him. "This is exactly what you need."

"A bunch of questions I don't want to answer?" Max returned dubiously. "I hardly think so."

"If you are going to move on with your life, you are going to have to face them sometime."

Max sighed, shaking his head. "I'm not sure this life is for me anymore. It's so . . . so empty."

His mother blanched. "How can you say that? It's been your dream for so long."

He loved to sing. There was no doubt about that. But the price he'd had to pay for it was far too high.

"What about Kelly?" he demanded harshly. "Does her death mean nothing to you?"

Ceilia gasped at his accusation. "How can you say that? She was my daughter. She—"

He put a hand on her arm to calm her. "Mum, I'm

sorry. I spoke without thought. I just . . ." He glanced back at the curtain. "I can't do this and pretend nothing ever happened."

His mother's lips thinned into a hard line. "No one is asking you to pretend *nothing ever happened.* But Kelly wouldn't have wanted you to give up your career, and you know it."

Max refused to answer. His mother was too idealistic. She didn't know what vultures lay in wait for him out there on the battleground she called a party. In a career like his, you always had to be on your toes. Anyone could be your enemy. No one was your friend, though many professed to be.

As a celebrity he was public property. And all they wanted to do was use him. The thought took him back to the worry that was never far from his thoughts. "How's security? Any reports of breaches?"

Ceilia sighed. "No, Max. Nor will there be." She put a tired hand on his arm. "Darling, your security people are on the outer wall and around the perimeter of the house, and we have helicopters flying overhead. I've even got the dogs patrolling the grounds."

"What dogs?"

"Cupid and Buttons."

"Cupid and Buttons! Those two would sell their souls to the devil for a pat on the head. . . ."

Ceilia put her hands on her hips defensively. "They will not. Miles has been training them for me on the weekends."

"Miles!" Max scoffed at the thought of his mother's

seventy-year-old gardener. "He's a bigger pushover than they are."

Ceilia seemed to realize that she couldn't argue with that and so hastily changed the subject. "Well, it doesn't matter. We have security everywhere. This place is Fort Knox. No one is going to get in."

He stuffed his hands into the pockets of his black suit pants. "You'd be surprised."

"Stop being so paranoid. The media can't reach you tonight. Nobody can. At least"—she grinned—"not without one of my coveted invitations."

He ignored her attempt at joviality. "Still, I'd like an update every hour. If those nosy leeches—"

"Don't even think about it," she returned crossly. "I will notify you if there is a breach, but there is no way that you're getting reports every hour. How are you supposed to relax and have fun?"

"I don't have any intention of doing either."

"Max!"

The tension slowly eased out of his face when he saw his mother's comical expression of horror.

"You never give up, do you?" he said.

"On my children?" She hugged him. "Never."

He shook his head, torn between affection and frustration.

"Look on the bright side, darling." She smiled. "Maybe you'll meet someone tonight. Someone special. Someone you might want to see again."

That statement, which seemed to come out of left field, startled him. "I beg your pardon?"

Her expression grew dreamy. "Wouldn't it be lovely if you met a nice girl and settled down to have children? You know it is my dearest wish that you should have the things in life that are the most important."

He looked at his mother as if she had just sprouted another head. "You've got to be kidding me. Meet someone?" He indicated behind him. "Here?"

Ceilia frowned. "Well, if you're going to be so negative about it, of course nothing will happen."

She looked so offended that he didn't have the heart to explain to her that superficial socialites on the lookout for an easy status boost didn't exactly make the best of wives. Despite her years, his mother was still such an innocent. And, God help him, he had never liked to upset her. She was the only real person left in his life now that Kelly was gone. The only person in his life who had loved him before all the glitz and glam.

"Mum . . ."

"Don't say it, love. Not tonight." She lifted her hands to smooth the lapels of his coat. "Tonight you are going to have a good time whether you want to or not." She crooked a finger, and with a sigh he bent down to her level so she could kiss him on the forehead.

"Happy Birthday, darling."

"Thanks, Mum," he grumbled.

Alexis crouched nervously behind the meter-high masonry retaining wall surrounding the foot of the mansion. The wall was lined with neatly manicured bushes.

All she had to do was creep along the wall till she hit the stone steps leading to the back entrance of the house. Up those steps and across a short patch of lawn was the French-door entrance to the lower level of Ceilia Deroux's mansion.

The problem was getting rid of the security guard standing right in front of it.

Alexis curled her fingers over the top of the wall and peered over it through a gap in the bushes. The guard was a burly individual dressed in a black uniform. He had one hand hooked over his belt in a kind of gangster stance. She could see the faint light at the end of his cigarette as he brought it to his lips and then exhaled deeply. She sank back behind the wall and bit her lip. There was no way to get around him. She had to get him to leave his post.

But how?

Alexis pulled her cell phone out of her pocket. Last year, when she was backpacking around Europe, she had used her phone as her alarm clock. She would set a time for a wake-up call when she was catching an early-morning flight. This time, the wake-up call would be for the security guard.

She set the alarm for 8:35 P.M., which was in exactly five minutes' time. Then she put the phone on a garden bench facing the lake in front of the wall. As quickly and soundlessly as she could, she slowly lay down on the top of the wall, still hidden from the security guard by the bushes. Lying flat on her belly, she inched to the forefront of the bushes. Just at that moment her phone began to ring. Ages ago she had changed the mundane manufacturer's ring tone to the rock song, "Wild Thing."

The rough number burst upon the silence of the night, every bit the wake-up call Alexis was looking for. She watched with satisfaction as the security guard immediately snapped to attention as if he'd been caught daydreaming. He threw his cigarette to the ground and stepped on it. As soon as it became apparent that he was still alone apart from the strange, insistent rocker's voice, he began to look about. Finally he did what Alexis really hoped he would do. He came forward, eyes alert, following the sound of the phone. He moved toward the top of the stone steps as the alarm grew louder. When she heard his footsteps descending, she jumped into action, leaping from the bushes, running across the grass and the short pavement to the French door, and then slipping inside just as the security guard was picking up her phone and answering it.

Luckily for Alexis, Sandra's expert computer skills had gotten them the floor plans of Ceilia Deroux's mansion a week ago. Alexis had memorized the entire layout, so she sped through the long corridors, dodging guards and house staff with the stealth of a professional or the luck of a Sunday born. She was inclined to think it was more the latter than the former. Nonetheless, she finally found herself in the foyer of the grand ballroom without any major hiccups. She scanned the room quickly to make sure the coast was clear and then dashed across the floor to the bathroom. She slipped inside and closed the door behind her, leaning back against it with relief.

I made it.

She allowed herself only a few seconds to catch her breath before unzipping the pouch strapped to her waist and pulling out a small sequined evening purse and some strappy black heels. She hung the purse on the back of the door and put the shoes on the floor. Unclipping the pouch strap, she let the bag drop to the floor.

Now for the transformation.

Pushing off her hood and pulling off her balaclava, she shook out her glossy black hair. It settled in waves down her back and across her shoulders. With shaky hands she unzipped her jumpsuit from neck to groin, peeled it off her shoulders, and stepped out of it, kicking it behind the toilet. She pulled down the short black evening dress bunched up around her waist till it swished appropriately just above her knees and then slipped her bare feet into the heels.

Okay.

Taking a deep breath, she grabbed her evening bag off the hook, picked up her pouch, and dropped it into the wastebasket. She caught sight of herself in the mirror before she exited the bathroom. It was not good.

The smoky eye makeup she had perfected earlier was a little smudged now. Luckily, it only took her a minute to repair the damage with a damp tissue. The effect certainly dressed up her little black cocktail dress. It made her brown eyes look mysterious—sexy, even. She withdrew a coral-colored gloss from her purse and touched up her lips.

All in all, she hoped she would pass. While elegant, her dress was no Gucci. It was a department-store bargain. The glittering stone at her throat was no diamond; it was zirconium, and so were the drops in her ears.

She looked at the watch that was definitely not from Switzerland.

9:05 P.M.

The night was still young. There was still time. All she needed was five minutes alone with him. Five minutes. Was that too much to ask? She ran trembling fingers through her ebony tresses, neatening the silky waves. It wasn't the way she'd thought she'd do it. But it wasn't as if she had options. This was the fastest way to impress the editor at *Starbuzz Magazine.* In any case, Deroux was a celebrity, a multimillionaire. What would five minutes of his time cost him, when it could make or break the lives of her sister's children?

Lifting her chin, she gave herself one last survey.

You can do this.

You must.

Alexis paused on the threshold and caught her breath. The ballroom was a haven of flowers and diamonds. The room glittered as the light from the giant crystal chandelier bounced off the wineglasses below. Ladies sparkling with jewels chatted carelessly with smartly dressed gentlemen in classic tuxedos. The heavenly smell of roses, orchids, and lilies filled Alexis' nostrils. They were everywhere, from table centers to buttonholes. Most of the guests were not unknown to her. She was going to be a nobody in a sea of celebrities. That thought immediately alerted her nerves.

How could she go unnoticed? Her very anonymity made her stand out. But it was too late for second thoughts or backing out. She would just have to make the best of it.

Even as she finished the thought, her attention was drawn to the rear of the room. The media's favorite matriarch, Ceilia Deroux, had just stepped out onto the center of a grand, horseshoe-shaped staircase. Her hand rested lightly on the sculptured stone railing that curved down around her as she surveyed the guests below.

Alexis hurried forward. Despite all her efforts, a little bubble of excitement burst behind her rib cage.

Oh, my gosh. It's about to happen. I'm actually going to see him. Max Deroux in the flesh.

It took all her concentration to stop a grin of glee from stretching her mouth. Her fingers curled into her palms, and she briefly closed her eyes to calm herself. He was just a man, after all.

Yeah, a man who's a singer, songwriter, and multimillionaire sex god.

"Ladies and gentlemen." Ceilia graciously called for the attention of her guests. "It is my great pleasure to announce that my son has finally arrived."

Alexis felt the excitement in the room heighten.

And then suddenly he was there.

Standing at the top of the stairs next to his mother, in all his glory. And glorious he was.

She had expected to be slightly disappointed. The media always built up celebrities too much. In the past she had found that, when confronted with the real deal, she often felt let down. They were always shorter or fatter in real life, lacking in personality or not as vibrant as they were on screen. But when Max Deroux sauntered into view, Alexis felt the floor drop out from under her feet.

He did not disappoint. If anything, he surpassed expectations.

Tall, dark, and handsome. He was the very embodiment of the cliché. Dressed in a black Armani suit with a collarless white shirt, he looked like the star he was. Gorgeous, elegant, charismatic, and seemingly unaware of it.

A kind of awed certainty came over Alexis as she stared up at him.

He is made for this.

He had that quality about him that you just had to be born with. He radiated allure. People were drawn to him, and she was annoyed to find that she was not immune to his powers.

Her eyes widened as the carefree smile that was his trademark curved his handsome mouth—that sexy twist of the lips that every woman in the room hoped he would throw their way. Herself included. She dropped her eyes to curb the feeling.

I can't afford to be attracted to him. I'm a journalist, not a fan. I'm here for a story, not an autograph.

A silence fell as the guests waited to hear what he would say.

"Thanks for waiting," he drawled.

A laugh and a cheer greeted this nonchalant sally. The band began to play the traditional birthday number that had the laughter continuing.

She lifted her eyes to see him whisper something into his mother's ear. Ceilia laughed and then watched him descend the stairs, as did every other eye in the room. Three beautiful women moved forward, racing one another to be the first to push a glass of Champagne into his hand.

It was then that reality began to set in. She was at the back of a crowd of celebrities all vying for his attention. How could she, a nobody, get to see him, much less talk to him and escape notice at the same time?

Her mission was impossible.

And then she thought about Kayla and Holly sitting on her threadbare couch, waiting for her to bring home a future. She couldn't fail them. She couldn't let her sister's children down. Not after everything they had been through.

Lifting her chin, she took a deep breath and strolled forward, weaving her way through the crowd with assurance. She ignored the stinging looks of the people she pushed in front of and maintained her path to her goal with quiet dignity. It was better not to talk to any of them. If she said anything, she would be open to questions, and she couldn't afford that.

At last she was almost at the base of the stairs, and she could see him. Tall, broad-shouldered, and effortlessly charismatic, he was unmistakable. His handsome head was bent to catch the teasing remark of a blond goddess in a red dress. Alexis's heart pattered wildly in her chest, but she suppressed it with outward calm.

He raised his head, and his steely gaze shot straight through her unseeingly before he turned back to his companion. She felt burned and breathless, even though she knew that he hadn't even registered her face. She looked at her hands, willing herself to get a grip. Now was not the time to be starstruck.

She peeped at others standing around her, watching him, waiting for their turn. It was going to be a nightmare getting to his side and even harder to hold his attention. She read the bored disinterest on his face as he spoke with Julia Evans, the actress voted last year as the World's Sexiest Woman by *Pop Magazine.* If that was his reaction to Julia Evans, what chance did Little Miss Nobody have?

Alexis swallowed.

Zero.

She was going to have to do something daring to get his attention.

She thought back to the jumpsuit in the bathroom, the Labradors eating steak, the fat guard answering her cell phone.

It wasn't as if she had any pride left to lose.

Alexis licked her lips, tossed her head, and veiled herself in an air of confidence.

Max Deroux was about to get the surprise of his life.

Chapter Two

"Julia." Max lifted his glass to acknowledge the stunning blond who had just kissed his cheek and tittered coyly, "Max, darling, it's been far too long."

As far as he was concerned, it had not been long enough. Julia was one of his more persistent admirers. A year ago he had found that amusing, even flattering. Now her sugary teasing grated on his nerves like fingernails against a blackboard. He really wasn't interested in her shallow perspective at all.

He scanned the room, exchanging nods with several people he knew but didn't want to talk to. A sinking feeling developed in his chest. There would be no shortage of prying questions tonight. Even as he thought it, he felt a hand under his chin as Julia eased his face back to hers.

"Oh, no, you don't," she pouted. "I've flown all the way from LA just to get your attention. Not to mention the effort I had to go to get this gown flown in from London to meet me here." She smoothed the slinky red fabric over her hips and did a little twirl for him. "You like?"

The barely-there gown was the embodiment of Hollywood beautiful, with a low back, minitrain, and scooped neckline that showed off her lovely collarbones, among other things.

"You look gorgeous as always, Julia."

"It's the least I could do for your birthday, Max." Her smile was ingratiating. "Are you enjoying yourself?"

"Immensely." He hoped the self-mockery in his voice wasn't too evident and then decided he didn't care.

"But do tell me, Max"—she trailed a finger up his arm—"where have you been hiding? I have been simply lost without you."

He studied the sparkling contents of his glass as he swirled it between thumb and forefinger. "Really? That surprises me."

She pouted. "Why?"

"Even I, on the odd occasion, have time to read the paper, Julia."

She had the grace to blush. He knew she had found another prize the minute he disappeared off the scene. In fact, the only reason she was probably here tonight was because that venture had failed.

"I can only assume you're referring to Daniel." Julia dismissed the lead singer of the rock band Catalyst with a wave of a French-manicured hand. "You shouldn't always believe what you read. I'm sure you of all people know that the tabloids are not to be trusted."

Max felt the smile fall off his face. He couldn't help it. There was, after all, a limit to his patience. Julia, however, seemed pleased that she had managed to unsettle him. She laid a sympathetic hand on his arm.

"Oh, darling, I'm sooo sorry. I didn't mean to bring it up. It's just that when you disappeared last year, I was so worried. More so, because I couldn't be there to comfort you as I wanted to."

He removed her hand from his arm. "Thank you for your concern, Julia. But I assure you, it was not needed."

In any way, shape, or form.

She looked down at her hands at that obvious snub and said somewhat tightly, "Perhaps you were getting comfort from someone else."

His sipped his Champagne, not deigning to reply to the churlish remark. She looked up, and he noticed that she had lost some of her beauty. Petulance didn't suit Julia at all.

"Perhaps from the woman you wrote that song about?" she pressed.

Max knew what song she was talking about but pretended he didn't and casually sipped his Champagne.

"What song?"

"The one on your album that's been in the Top Ten practically all year. You know, 'Blue Angel.' "

He felt as if he had written that song an age ago, even though it was only about a year. It was the last song he had released. He had been a completely different man back then. He smiled cynically. Amazing, how your life could change in an instant.

"Are you seeing someone, Max? Who is your Blue Angel?"

His eyes refocused on her pensive countenance, and he wondered whether to string her along or put her out of her misery. But before he could reply, a sultry voice at his elbow did it for him.

"That would be me."

What the . . . ?

He felt an arm go around his waist and turned left just in time to receive a soft kiss on the lips.

"Hi, Max."

His eyes locked with a pair of sinful chocolate pools, enticingly smudged with black eyeliner and framed in the longest lashes he'd ever seen. She took the Champagne in his hand and sipped it, watching him over the rim. He continued to stare back at her, completely poleaxed by those "baby don't cry" eyes.

It wasn't to say that many women hadn't tried to seduce him in the past. Hell, when she could, Julia made it her full-time job. But he had never felt the slightest urge to succumb to any of them . . . until now.

Slowly she lowered the glass and pushed it back into his unresisting hand. She tossed her head, and her glossy hair feathered across her shoulders and whisked about her heart-shaped face.

"So sorry I'm late," she murmured. "You know how it is."

It was Julia who spoke first, if somewhat irritably. "I don't believe we've been introduced."

The woman did not break their gaze as she replied, "Alexis Banks."

She said the name as if it should mean something to Julia. But Julia didn't rise to the bait. Alexis sighed and turned fully to the woman who was only one of Hollywood's biggest actresses. She held out her hand as the queen might to a lowly subject. "Julia, isn't it?" Her lips curled with faint surprise. "I thought you'd be in Vegas with Daniel."

Max saw the brief flash of rage cross Julia's face before it was replaced with a smile that was as hard as nails. She gave Alexis's hand the briefest of shakes.

"Actually, Daniel and I—"

But Alexis had already turned her body into his again and was staring up into his eyes with mesmerizing effect. She didn't allow Julia to finish and said without turning, "If you don't mind, I'm just going to borrow my other half for minute." Her smile held the promise of paradise. "I need to give him his birthday present."

Alexis felt as if her heart was beating inside her head when she turned to lead Max Deroux from the room. His large hand was tucked snugly into hers, their fingers intimately laced together, the taste of Champagne she had shamelessly sipped from his glass still lingered on her lips. And yet . . . he had offered no resistance. He had not said a word in protest.

I can't believe I just did that. I can't believe he's coming with me. I can't believe—

"Where are you taking me?"

She stopped.

Yeah, where are you taking him?

She turned around to meet dancing blue eyes. A tickle of awareness skittered down her spine. Man, he was gorgeous. "I don't know." She lowered her voice, trying to keep it even, but it came out husky. "Where can we be alone?"

His eyes seemed to widen. "Direct, aren't you?"

"I need to talk to you."

He inclined his head. "I admit, you have me curious. How about my mother's library? It's . . . empty."

She hesitated. How deep was she getting? "Where is it?"

"I can take you there."

He squeezed her hand, and a ripple of pleasure shot up her arm. "Come on, we'd better go before *someone* tries to stop us." His mouth stretched into a full grin, and she couldn't help but return his mischievous smile. It was real, not the stuck-on curl of the lips he had given Julia. He looked as if for the first time that evening he was actually having some fun. Well, good for him. It was the least she could do in return for what she needed. She felt her heart tighten in guilt. Why did he have to be such a nice guy?

Max led the way through the crowd, nodding firmly at people who tried to stop them. As she followed in the protection of his wake, Alexis shook off the spell he had cast over her. She had to get out of la-la land and focus on what she was there for. So far she had been lucky enough to get him to lead her out of the crowd. But keeping him by her side was going to take skill. The most important thing of all, of course, was capturing it all on tape. Keeping her eyes on his back, she inconspicuously dipped her hand into her evening bag. Feeling around, her trembling fingers soon stumbled upon the tiny tape recorder there. She pressed down the Record button and removed her hand just as Max whisked her out of the ballroom and into the foyer.

They walked down a short, dimly lit hall and then took a left into the double-doored entrance of a dark room. She could just make out shadows of sofas and a coffee table. The shape of a lamp adorned a cabinet across the room, and Max released her hand to go turn it on. Light illuminated her surroundings, and she saw that the walls were actually lined from floor to ceiling with bookshelves. There was no pattern to the titles; they ranged from modern science to classical English literature. She would love a collection like this. As Alexis studied the rows of books with undisguised awe, Max sat down in a leather armchair, right ankle over left, and studied her.

Max liked what he saw.

Alexis Banks was a gorgeous mix of innocence and allure, big eyes and a kissable mouth. Her beauty was natural rather than fabricated. He didn't recognize the style of her designer but had a sneaky suspicion it wouldn't matter who made her clothes. Alexis had that elusive talent that so many women in the ballroom behind them hankered after: She made her clothes look good, not the other way around. The black dress accentuated a figure that Max could only describe as perfection. Gently rounded shoulders, a tiny waist, curvaceous hips, and long, *long* legs.

"Like what you see?"

She said the words before she slowly turned her head to look at him. It made his shoulders shake with silent mirth. Damn women and their peripheral vision. She had clearly witnessed his admiration under the guise of studying his mother's collection. Or perhaps the multi-talented Alexis was doing both. There was no use being coy, so he decided to be frank, lacing his fingers in his lap.

"You know I do. Otherwise, why would I have allowed you to lure me away from my own birthday party under false pretenses?"

She put a hand on one slender hip. "You weren't enjoying it."

"You don't know that."

She rolled her eyes and walked toward the bookshelf on her left. "Puh-lease, I saw the way you were looking at Julia Evans. Not that I blame you. You know, I have never understood why people go to see her movies. They've all got the same plot."

"Which is?"

"Girl meets boy. Girl acts dumb. Boy patronizes girl. Girl wears a bikini. Boy asks girl to marry him. Girl wears bikini one last time. Then they get married."

Max laughed.

"Am I right, or am I right?"

He said nothing.

"Admit it, you were as bored as a cheese platter out there."

Max coughed to hide his smile. "I've been called many things in my career but never a cheese platter."

She pulled a volume from the shelf in front of her. Flipping it over, she held it to her chest. His eyes ran over the cover of the classic novel by Charles Dickens, *Great Expectations.*

"Have you read this?"

"No."

"You should."

She placed the book back on the shelf and trailed her fingers across the titles beside it.

Max sat forward. "So, what is it you want to talk about?"

She sashayed toward him, dropping her handbag on the table by his elbow and walking behind his chair. She brushed her fingerstips across his shoulders, leaving a trail of fire in their wake.

Just as she would have passed him, he turned around and snatched her wrist. "Stop that! Or you'll get more than you bargained for."

"Let me go."

He looked up into her face and was surprised to see fear there for the first time. Satisfied, he let her go and indicated the chair opposite him.

"Sit down. I want to know exactly what your game is, sweetheart. And I want to know right now."

Alexis knew it was time to stop stalling. If she was going to do this properly, she was going to have to use her brain, not her feminine wiles. Her original intention had been to subtly interview him at the party—you know, take him a glass of Champagne and introduce herself as one of his mother's friends. It would have been casual, cool, and delightfully unsuspicious. Of course that plan had been squashed the minute she'd seen the crowd and at least a dozen others with almost exactly the same idea. She needed an excuse for having dragged him away, and it had to be believable. But what could she say? What important matter would not only keep him by her side but help facilitate an interview?

She couldn't tell him she was a journalist. Hell's fire would immediately rain down on her if she so much as mentioned the media. She'd be kicked out the door in short order, probably with a lawsuit snapping at her heels. She had read enough tabloids to know that Max Deroux hated reporters. Not just mildly, but passionately, with every fiber of his being. Not that he didn't have just cause. If she were in his shoes . . .

But she wasn't in his shoes, was she? She was in her own. And her shoes were a lot tighter and a lot more uncomfortable. His issues were all about the past. Hers were very much in the present. And if she didn't slip into the mindset and fast, she was going to lose the one opportunity she desperately needed.

Moving toward the couch, she did as he suggested and sat down, crossing one leg over the other. "The matter I need to discuss is personal," she said softly.

"Why the charade?"

"I didn't want to talk about this with you in the ballroom. I didn't want Julia Evans or anyone else, for that matter, being a party to it."

"Why didn't you just say so?"

"Would you have come with me if I had merely asked you?"

His lips twitched. "Probably not."

"Then you know why I did it."

"Okay then." Max spread his hands invitingly. "You have my attention."

Alexis swallowed as she realized what a lie she would have to embark upon. It was underhanded. But what other choice did she have? It was the only story she could think of that would not only help her get her interview but was still believable as a cover. She had to use it. The alternative of being exposed was unthinkable.

"It's about your sister," she began.

Max seemed to still as she uttered the fatal last word. The sparkle dropped out of his eyes, and his handsome mouth thinned. "You knew her?"

Alexis froze. She didn't want to lie outright, so she said instead, "Kelly was a wonderful person."

He looked away, not meeting her eyes. "I'm sorry, but Kelly's death is one subject not open to discussion."

Alexis sat forward. "When I heard what happened . . ."

Max stood up, and this time he walked to the bookshelves, keeping his back to her. "Kelly's been dead for over a year. You can't have only just heard about it."

"No." Alexis bit her lip and racked her brain. Then her eyes fluttered back to him more confidently. "I've known for months, but as you must know, you haven't exactly made yourself available. It's only just now that I've been able to get a hold of you."

"To tell me what?" Max demanded, spinning around in a sudden burst of anger. "That you're sorry? I know you're sorry. Everybody's sorry. There's not a damn person in this world who wasn't sorry to see her go."

He ran frustrated fingers through his dark locks before crossing the room. She felt the hurt radiating from his being, as if she could reach out and touch it.

"I know what you're going through."

"No, you don't," Max snapped. "And, for the record, Kelly's never spoken about you, ever."

"There's a lot of things about Kelly you don't know, Max." Alexis took a risk. "But you shouldn't beat yourself up about it. You can never really know every single thing there is to know about a person. They let different people into their lives at different times and in different ways."

He was silent, still refusing to look at her.

"Max." She stood up.

He turned around. "Look, you may have known my sister, but you don't know me." His features were stretched taut with pain, and her heart leaped out to him. His demons were sitting all around him. They looked so familiar to her own. She just wanted to stretch out her hand and touch her palm to his cheek. Tell him it was okay. Tell him he wasn't alone.

"I know she wouldn't want you to grieve like this."

His jaw loosened, and he looked up, shaking his head. "My mother put you up to this, didn't she?"

"No." Alexis walked forward. "I just know what it's like. I've lost . . ." She stopped in confusion.

"You've lost what?"

Alexis sighed, meeting his eyes with a kind of desperate yearning. "I've lost a sister too. Just recently actually. A . . . uh . . . a couple of months ago."

That confession stopped him in his tracks. It stopped her too. She had never meant to tell him that. Why had she? For a moment they stood in silence, until she shrugged off the awkwardness with her usual spunk.

"What? You're not going to tell me you're sorry?"

She walked beside the bookshelves, running her fingers along the polished shelving. "We were going out for dinner—Mel, her husband, their twin girls and me. It was her birthday. I hadn't seen her in months because I'd been backpacking around Europe all winter." She felt the tears welling and hastily blinked them away. Taking a deep breath, she continued. "I suggested this restaurant in Paddington. It was an Italian place we'd been meaning to check out before I'd left for London but hadn't had a chance to. I waited there for at least two hours, thinking they were late. But—" She stopped and put her fingers to her lips to stop them from trembling. "I wasn't to see my sister that night, or my brother-in-law. They were . . . in an accident with a bus. Apparently the driver was drunk at the wheel."

"Oh, hell."

Alexis threw Max a brief glance. "Understatement." She paused to gather the strength to continue. "My sister and her husband were killed instantly. The front of the car took the worst of the impact. I saw my nieces later that night at the hospital. Kayla and Holly both had broken bones and cuts. Luckily, nothing too serious." She hastily brushed aside a tear that had leaked out of her eye.

"Are they okay now?"

She hadn't realized it, but while she had been finishing her story, Max had crossed the room to her side. He was no more than a few feet from her, his face the very picture of concern.

"Yes." Her smile was watery. "But I'm not." She folded her arms protectively over her chest and looked up at him with wide, frightened eyes. "I'm scared to death."

"Why?"

"I'm twenty-four years old, Max. What do I know about raising children? I can barely look after myself."

His mouth curved. "From what I've seen of you, you can definitely look after yourself."

She rolled her eyes and looked away, causing him to move till he was standing directly in front of her. Taking her firmly by the shoulders he said, "You can do this."

Even though he barely knew her, Max knew he meant every word he was saying. He had never met a woman who could take him so high and then floor him in the next heartbeat. She was something else. Something he couldn't define and didn't want to. She was special, and it was important to him that she knew that.

"You don't know me at all," she said as though to echo his thoughts.

He smiled. "I know that when you walk into a room, you own it. I know that you're smart, savvy, and you don't take no for an answer, and I know that my sister liked you, which in itself speaks volumes."

That remark seemed to make her uncomfortable, and she shrugged off his hands and moved back toward the couch.

"Did Kelly ever talk about me?" he asked softly.

She threw him a coy smile as she reseated herself on the couch. "Everybody talks about you, Max. How talented you are. How gorgeous you are. Don't you ever get sick of hearing about yourself?"

He laughed and joined her on the sofa. "Yes."

Do I ever.

"But they're right, you know. You have a beautiful voice."

He grimaced. "Fame has its price."

"I assume you're talking about Kelly."

"The biggest price of all."

"It wasn't your fault."

He met the troubled eyes of the beautiful woman sitting across from him, and for the first time in a long while he felt safe, at ease. This gorgeous, brave woman had just unburdened herself to him, and he wanted to do the same, open up to her. Let all the anger in him out, so that he could move on with his life. Feel free again.

"That's where you're wrong." He looked at his hands. "I remember that day as clearly as yesterday. It was after a big concert, and Kelly was going to meet me out back. The limo was going to pick us up there. It was late, and the media got wind of the fact that I'd be coming out the back entrance of the club. Kelly was standing by the roadside when I came out the door. She was yelling a warning to me. I saw some camera guy push her aside to get to me first. She fell back onto the road. I saw the car hit her. I saw it. I saw it with my own eyes." His fingers curled into fists. "I still see it sometimes in nightmares."

He felt a hand on his shoulder, and he glanced up at the woman beside him.

"That still doesn't make it your fault."

"Do you honestly think if I hadn't been so caught up with my fans and my singing and all that nonsense that my sister wouldn't still be alive today?"

She paused. "Do you honestly think that if I hadn't chosen that Italian restaurant, my sister would still be alive today?"

He shook his head. "That's different."

"How is it different?" she demanded. "You can ask as many what-ifs as you like. The fact is, it wasn't in your control. You can't determine what other people do. All you can do is live your life to the best of your ability."

"But I didn't," Max argued. "I let all that fame rubbish get to me. I let it rule my life. I should have been more vigilant. I should have paid more attention to the media."

"Max, the media isn't going to get any less persistent. It doesn't matter how vigilant you are."

He put his head in his hands. "I just wish I could rewind the clock."

"Max," Alexis insisted, "singing is your life. Don't give it up because of some misplaced desire to punish yourself."

Max shrugged. "I wouldn't know what to sing about even if I could. Kelly was my muse. With her gone . . ."

"Get a new one."

He gave her a wry grin. "I guess there's always that. But who?"

"I don't know. Who do you know?" She shrugged her creamy shoulders, and he couldn't help but be drawn to the gentle movement.

Suddenly it wasn't about who he knew but who was right in front of him.

What about her?

The amazing woman he had just bared his soul to. How did she do that? How did she make everything seem so simple? She too seemed to sense his change of mood, veiling her eyes with impossibly long lashes and licking her lips nervously. Man, she was gorgeous. Rip-out-your-heart beautiful. He should be concentrating on why she was here, on why she wanted to talk about Kelly. But the need to get to know her seemed more pressing.

"Alexis."

She glanced at him uncertainly. "Yes?"

"What do you know about music?" He lifted a hand to cup her cheek.

He felt her sharp intake of her breath as he bent his head slowly toward hers. He wanted to catch those cherub lips she had teased him with not so long ago.

An awkward cough interrupted them. "Excuse me, sir."

Damn!

Mere millimeters from her upturned mouth, Max was forced to pull away. In turn, she sat back, red with embarrassment. Max glanced over his shoulder at the door behind them.

A security guard stood on the threshold.

"So sorry to interrupt, sir. But you asked me to come and see you at once if there was a security breach."

Max stood up. "And is there?"

"Sir"—the guard looked worried—"I think we have an intruder."

He lifted his hands, and Max spied the three items he was holding.

A black jumpsuit, a pouch, and a mobile phone.

Chapter Three

*O*h, *crap.*

As inconceivable as it was, Alexis had managed to forget who she was until the evidence was literally thrust under her nose. Max seemed to have this unnerving ability to make her throw caution to the winds, make her fears look like anthills instead of mountains. Perhaps it was because he treated her as if she was somebody— spoke to her as if her opinion mattered—looked at her as if she was worth knowing. It was ridiculous, really. What did she have to show for her life, except a lot of unfinished goals and a stack of bills she couldn't pay?

As the guard held up her belongings for Max's closer inspection, she realized that being poor and dysfunctional was the least of her problems. Right now keeping her butt out of jail was a higher priority.

"Wow." She swallowed, looking from Max to the security guard and then back again. "Maybe I should go."

"No, no." Max waved a hand at her as she moved to get her purse. "This won't take a moment." He turned back to the security guard. "Has anyone seen this intruder?"

"Actually, I would feel better if—" Alexis tried again, but the security guard was speaking at the same time.

"No, but we have all exits patrolled. No one is leaving this place without identifying themselves first."

Alexis decided to shut up. *Well, there goes getting out undetected.*

She might as well stay and find out if there were going to be any gaps in security.

"I knew something like this would happen." Max swore. "The bloody media will stop at nothing. Let me see that."

He stuck out a hand for the jumpsuit, and the guard handed it to him. Alexis held her breath as he spread the outfit between his hands, feeling the material and measuring it for size.

"It's a woman," he muttered, and he looked up. "Where is my mother?"

"I believe she is still in the ballroom with the rest of the guests, and also, we assume, the intruder," the guard replied, taking back the jumpsuit. "Mrs. Deroux hasn't been notified of the situation yet, sir."

"I see." Max paced for a moment.

Alexis watched him, her lower lip taking the brunt of her nervous energy. When his feet suddenly stopped, it took all her concentration not to jump.

"I can't stay here," Max announced. "I'm not going back into the ballroom with a bloody journalist skulking about."

"It could be a fan," Alexis suggested tentatively.

But the look he threw at her was adamant. "Believe me, it's a journalist." He turned back to the guard. "Will you notify my mother that I've left, and have my driver bring the car around the front please?"

"Yes, sir."

Max turned to Alexis. "Do you want to come?"

"Come?" Alexis squeaked.

"You want to go back in there?" He indicated the ballroom behind the wall.

"Er . . ." Alexis ran an agitated hand through her hair. "Um . . ."

The problem wasn't going back to the ballroom; it was getting out of it. If all the exits were now patrolled . . . Maybe she *should* go with him. At least that would secure her safe passage out of the house.

Max seemed to have misinterpreted her indecision, because he lightly touched her shoulder, sending her a smile that made her bones melt. "Just for coffee, Alexis."

She glanced at the security guard, who looked away, pretending he hadn't noticed the tension in the room.

"Okay," she agreed.

"The car should be by the front entrance in five minutes, sir."

"Thank you."

* * *

The entrance to Ceilia's mansion was patrolled by six security guards. Alexis hurried down the steps with her hand tucked inside Max's and thanked God that she had accepted his offer. There was no way she could have slipped undetected past six trained men. She was smart, but she wasn't that smart.

The driver opened the door to a white limousine parked at the base of the steps. Max indicated that she should go first. Alexis eased across the white leather seat, eyeing the bottle of Champagne already open in the silver wine cooler in front of her. She wondered how many women Max had taken for a ride in this fancy car and then stopped herself on the thought. What did it matter anyway? It wasn't as if she was one of his Hollywood babes vying for a date.

She rubbed her arms as goose bumps appeared. If he knew who she was . . . She shuddered.

He would kill her.

And that wasn't a figure of speech. Not that she would blame him. Man, after breaking and entering into his mother's house, pretending to know his sister—his tragically deceased sister, mind you—who wouldn't take the death penalty into their own hands? She gripped her arms till her knuckles turned white. Who had she become, using a death in someone's family as a means to her own end? She shook her head in disgust. She should be shot. This was beyond shameful. It was macabre.

"Hey, are you okay?"

She glanced at the man seated across from her, his arm up on the back of the seat. Behind him she could see that they had left the mansion already and were out on the main road. Absorbed in her own regret, she hadn't even noticed they had taken off.

"Yeah." She forced a smile onto her lips. "Fine."

"Thought we'd go to Crusades."

Crusades!

She had never dreamed that she would ever set foot in there. The ritzy six-star restaurant wasn't even slightly in her league. But it did make sense that the local coffee shop was out of the question when you were Max Deroux.

"Sure." She swallowed. But her tension made her bones ache, and her nails dug into the palms of her clenched hands.

I can't do this anymore. It's too much.

She couldn't use the man like this.

He was a good man.

A kind, sensitive, generous man.

She couldn't publish his pain, use his suffering to earn herself a living, no matter how desperately she needed the money. It was madness to have concocted this scheme in the first place. He didn't deserve that.

No one did.

"Are you sure you're okay?"

She looked at him for a long moment, the moonlight glinting off his dark hair, the sexy smile like forbidden fruit sitting temptingly on his masculine mouth. Her decision crystallized.

"Yeah, I'm sure."

* * *

Something had changed. Max didn't know what it was, but it was holding Alexis back. The minx in the ballroom was gone, and the compassionate woman he'd confided in back at the library had retreated behind a wall. He couldn't figure out for the life of him what he'd said to offend her. But whatever it was, she was clearly not going to give him the opportunity to take it back. They arrived at the hotel with no more than a few sentences between them, mostly about the weather.

Her guard was up big-time, and it was going to take every drop of his personality to draw her out again. The driver came around to open the door. Max saw the faint flash of a distant camera as he stepped out and immediately shielded Alexis from view. He was not going to have her life ruined by being drawn into the mess that was his. They quickly ran up the marble steps and into the hotel, alarming the concierge with the sudden celebrity occupancy. He hurried forward.

"Mr. Deroux! Good evening."

"We'd like to go up to Crusades if you don't mind, Harry."

"Of course, sir."

The concierge led them to the elevators. When the door of the one farthest to the left opened, he swiped his security key over the operation panel and pressed the button for the top floor. Max and Alexis stepped in, and the doors slid closed behind them. Max studied Alexis. His eyes slid over her rigid body as she kept her own gaze firmly on the door. What was bothering her? He decided to try conversation again.

"Ever been to Crusades before?"

She shook her head. "No."

"My mother loves it." He paused. "I expect Kelly told you that."

She looked up at him then. "Max—"

The doors slid open, and he stepped out into the lobby of the plush restaurant owned and run by French chefs.

She caught his arm as he was about to lead her inside. "Max, I think I might pass on coffee."

He turned back, his eyes widening with surprise. "Why?"

She bit her lip. "I . . . I have a headache."

"You have a headache." He looked up at the ceiling. "Well, if that's not a blow to my ego, I don't know what is."

"Max." She squeezed his arm, and he looked down again. "Don't take this personally. I just need to go, that's all."

"Alexis," he said softly. "If you don't tell me what's wrong, how can I help?"

"Nothing is wrong." She lifted her chin and shook her head, her luscious hair whisking about her shoulders.

It was all he could do not to reach out and run his fingers through it. "What did I say to offend you?"

"Nothing. I just need to go home. The twins need me."

The children. Realization dawned on him. "Of course. Let me take you."

Again she stayed him. "No."

"Come on. I'll take you home."

"No, Max."

He stopped and looked at her wonderingly. What he would do for five seconds inside that stubborn little head of hers. What was she so worried about?

"Alexis . . ."

"I mean it, Max." Her smile seemed forced. "You go in and enjoy yourself. I'll catch a cab."

Short of taking her off by force, it looked as if he couldn't change her mind. He couldn't really argue any further without appearing rude or overbearing.

"All right, if you're sure," he reluctantly agreed. "But I can't say I'm happy about it."

She nodded and held out her hand. "I'm sure. It was great meeting you . . . really."

He looked at the small, delicate hand in front of him, and a sudden desperation seized him. "Wait." He grasped the hand between both of his. "That can't be it."

She looked up at him, her expression confused.

He searched her face. He'd just found her. He couldn't let her go just like that. "Alexis, I want to see you again."

If it were possible, her eyes seemed to grow larger. Slowly but firmly she withdrew her hand. "Max, you don't know what you're saying."

"I'm just asking you out on a date, Alexis."

"And I appreciate it, but—"

"Look," he began, "I've never connected with someone as quickly as I have with you tonight. I don't want that to end. I want to see you again."

She sighed. "Max, you don't want to go out with me. It wouldn't work."

"Why not? Is it because I'm a celebrity?"

She winced. "In part."

His heart sank. *Bloody fame; it never failed to fail him.*

"I guess I can't change who I am, Alexis, but I'm a lot more flexible than I used to be." He grimaced as he recalled his life before Kelly died. He had been a slave to his own success, sometimes at the exclusion of all else. Boy, had he learned his lesson!

But this comment didn't seem to appease her. "You don't understand," she refuted. "It's not that. It's just . . . there are things about me you don't know."

"Alexis, at this point I can't think of anything you could tell me that would put me off wanting to see you again."

"I can," she muttered darkly.

He sighed. Was there no getting through to her? "Didn't you feel the chemistry between us tonight?" he demanded. "Didn't you—" He reached out toward her, and she took a giant step backward.

Okay, bad move.

He dropped his hands.

"I felt it," she replied shortly. "And that's why I'm doing you a favor. I'm not the woman for you, Max. Not by a long shot."

The elevator doors opened behind them, and the Prime Minister walked in with his wife. He tipped his head briefly at Max as he passed through to the restaurant. Max watched in frustration as Alexis took the opportunity to step backward into the elevator. He stuck his palm on one of the doors before they could close.

"Look," he tried one last time. "On the off chance that

you change your mind, which I hope you do, I want you to take this." He reached into his pocket and pulled out his wallet. Withdrawing a business card from within, he held it out to her and added, "It's my private number."

She studied the card in his hand and finally, with a sigh, took it.

He grabbed her wrist as her hand withdrew. "Promise me you'll think about it."

She nodded reluctantly. "I'll think about it."

"Okay then." He released her wrist and stepped back. The doors slid closed.

Alexis bit back tears all the way home.

That beautiful idiot of a man.

Why did he have to be so wonderful? It made her guilt that much worse. The fact that he was as attracted to her as she was to him couldn't help but affect her. It exalted and humiliated her at the same time. There was nothing more wrong or more right about it. If only things were different. If only she hadn't dug such a huge hole for herself; she needed another grappling hook to get out . . .

She could just imagine their dinner conversation if they did go out.

"So, what do you do?"

"I'm a journalist."

"Oh, so are you going to stab me in the back now or later?"

"Nah, I already did that when I jumped your mother's

fence, lied to you about your dead sister, and then had the audacity to go on a date with you."

"Wow, and I thought that jerk who pushed my sister in front of the car was bad."

Alexis put her head in her hands.

Who am I kidding?

I'm an idiot.

And dating Max Deroux would take *idiot* to a whole new level. She'd have to pile lies on top of lies just to get by. Unless she told the truth, the whole truth. She swallowed. He'd probably hate her even more. As wonderful as he was, it was better if she cut all ties before she hurt him further.

Wasn't it?

She shook off the uncertainty. Max Deroux, despite his gorgeous perfectness, was not a priority.

The twins were.

She would have to find another way to make money to support them. And fast. But one thing was for sure. She couldn't raise the twins on blood money, and she should have realized that from the start.

Finally, the taxi reached her home in Hornsby. She had taken the cab from the train station. A cab all the way from central Sydney would have cost her an arm and a leg. Completing her journey in two stages had been much cheaper. Money wasn't something Alexis could take for granted. Rent alone consumed eighty percent of her income, since she'd had to ask her old roommate to leave to make room for the twins. Not that her old, weathered-board house was anything to be envied. Its ragged exterior was in serious need of renovation. The inside was liveable but small. In any event, the house certainly wasn't ideal, especially for kids.

She paid the driver and tried not to groan as she exited the vehicle. A dull light illuminated a front window of the house. She trampled across the weed-infested lawn and up the old porch steps to her front door. Unlocking it, she stepped into a living room that was retro by age, not design.

Sandra was seated on a brown and orange couch that had seen better days, sipping a cup of hot tea. She had removed her black catsuit and was wearing a white shirt and blue jeans. Her brown hair was pulled back into a ponytail that seemed to accentuate the sharp angles of her face.

"Where are the twins?" Alexis asked.

"In bed." Sandra dismissed them with a wave of her hand. "But never mind about that. Tell me! Did you get it?"

It was clear that Sandra's mind was focused on only one thing. Alexis frowned at her, dropping her handbag and keys onto the kitchen counter. It was difficult enough trying to get a handle on the parent thing without people dismissing your newfound role left, right, and center as though it didn't matter.

"Yes," Alexis sighed. "But do you have to be so one-track minded? I think I'll check on the twins first."

She left the room. Sandra's attitude seemed to be getting more and more mercenary of late. Perhaps it was better she got out of the business before it was too late.

Sandra was right. The twins were sleeping sweetly in their beds when she checked on them. Kayla had kicked off her blankets, so Alexis picked them up off the floor and tucked them around her shoulders. She stirred briefly but didn't wake up. Alexis' heart ached as her gaze swept over Kayla's little face. Blond hair, cherub cheeks, and small round shoulders. She was so innocent, so vulnerable. Alexis hoped that she could be the mother her sister needed her to be.

When she emerged from the twins' bedroom, she found Sandra still sitting on the couch but now listening to her tape recorder. Clearly, she had fished it out of Alexis' purse without a please or thank you. Alexis was beginning to feel just a little violated. Sandra might be her only way into *Starbuzz Magazine,* but that didn't give her the right to go through her personal things.

Alexis walked to the coffee table, snatched up the tape recorder, and pressed Stop. She looked down at Sandra seated on the couch, so the woman could not mistake her anger.

"What?" Sandra lowered her mug. "You took a while, so I just thought I'd get a head start."

Alexis gritted her teeth. "How dare you go through my things? That was a private conversation."

"Private?" Sandra laughed. "Alex, that stuff is gold. I tell you what—there is no way the senior editor is going to turn down your application when I present her with your article on Max Deroux."

"I'm not writing it anymore. I can't use this."

"What!" Sandra put down her mug and stood up. "You can't be serious."

"I've never been more serious about anything in my life." She popped the tape out and put the recorder back on the coffee table. "This"—she held up the evidence—"is not going into *Starbuzz Magazine*. It is exactly what I said, a private conversation."

"Are you mad?" Sandra put her cup down on the table. "I thought you needed a job. I can't give you a recommendation if I've got nothing to impress the senior editor with."

"You know what? I'm beginning to think that *Starbuzz* is not the place for me after all."

"Look, Alex, you don't have to mention anything about you or your sister or her kids in the article."

"But it's okay to exploit his sister and her death?" Alexis threw at her. "Isn't that just a bit hypocritical? I won't do it, Sandra. I don't want the job that much."

Sandra put her hands on her hips. "You didn't have a problem with it yesterday."

"I was too caught up in my own issues, in the twins, in our needs."

I was too much like you.

Alexis winced guiltily as she remembered Max's words.

The bloody media will stop at nothing.

Was that who she was? Was that what she had become? She couldn't let that happen. She shook her head.

"Look, the point is, I couldn't see the forest for the trees."

Sandra's jaw dropped an inch, and her eyes looked heavenward. "And now you can?"

"He's a good guy, Sandra. He doesn't deserve this. Nobody does."

"Okay, so now that you're all noble and everything, how are you going to support the twins? Your Social Security allowance is a joke. Without a job—"

"Don't you think I know that?"

Alexis looked away. After she'd settled her brother-in-law's debts, there had been next to nothing left for the twins' future. She desperately needed a steady income.

"What are you going to do, Alexis? You can't keep the kids in this dump forever. This year they start school. Freelancing pays peanuts unless you have the big story everybody wants."

"I'll find another story." Alexis shrugged.

"Well, I'm not." Sandra stood up and lunged forward. It was only Alexis' quick reflexes that enabled her to step back before Sandra snatched the tape out of her hand.

"Hey!" she cried, eyeing the hard-nosed reporter's frenzied expression with growing trepidation.

"You may be willing to give up this godsend," Sandra cried, "but I'm not. Give that to me."

"No way."

Sandra's lips tightened over clenched teeth, and Alexis knew that if she didn't do something fast, it was going to end very badly. She broke the tape in half.

Sandra gasped as Alexis dropped it into a nearby wastebasket.

"Sorry, Sandra. I meant it when I said this tape is not going to be used."

Sandra looked down at the bin and then back at her. Alexis had to step away from the fury that radiated from her.

"I can't believe you just did that. How can you throw away such a brilliant story?"

"My sister trusted me with those kids." Alexis shook her head. "She trusted me to do the right thing, and I'm not going to disappoint her for a quick-fix solution."

And I'm not going to betray Max either.

"You're making a big mistake," Sandra hissed as Alexis started to walk away.

"Look, Sandra, it's late, and I've had rough night. I know you had your hopes set on this. But don't worry, you'll get another story. Just not from me."

Sandra looked away, and Alexis ground her teeth, wondering how she was going to get through to her. She hadn't known Sandra long, but she knew stubbornness when she saw it. Suddenly they both heard a small cry from the twins' bedroom.

"Aunty Alex?"

One of the girls had woken up. Sandra rolled her eyes, and Alex sighed. "I need to check on her."

She quickly ducked into the twins' bedroom again to find Kayla sitting up in bed.

"I had a bad dream."

Alexis sat down beside her and brushed Kayla's hair out of her face. "It's over now, sweetie."

It took a good ten minutes to get Kayla back under the covers. When Alexis returned to the kitchen, she noticed that Sandra had left. Her brain was so dulled with relief that she wouldn't have to deal with Sandra anymore, she didn't stop to question what Sandra might have taken in her silent retreat.

Instead, she returned to the counter to pick up her black purse. As she moved it, Max's card fell out. She lifted it off the counter and held it between thumb and forefinger. Tingles rippled down her arm. The man had the power to affect her even without his presence. She shivered as the bold black numbers on the card taunted her.

Dare I?

Unbidden, the memory of Max's imploring blue eyes materialized in her mind's eye. It had taken all her willpower to step back into that elevator. Yet his words still teased at the edges of her frayed mind.

Promise me you'll think about it?

Hell, she was thinking about it all right. There were no issues there. The problem was resisting it. Max was a hard man to just forget. Sure, she'd had her share of dates in the past, heard just about every pickup line in existence when she was travelling though Europe. But never had a guy swept her off feet the way Max had. He seemed to know her without knowing her.

He was perfect.

She walked into the living room, staring at the card till her knees hit the side of the couch. She sank unconsciously onto its soft cushions.

What if she told him the truth? What if she confessed everything? What if she just laid it all out on the table?

Would he forgive her?

Would he understand why she'd done it? What she had at stake?

Again his words came back to her, taunting her with hope.

Alexis, at this point I can't think of anything you could tell me that would put me off wanting to see you again.

She bit her lip. Did she let him go or take a chance on pure, old-fashioned honesty?

Finally she tore her gaze from the card and lowered it to her lap. It was worth the risk, wasn't it? Since when had Alexis Banks ever backed away from a challenge? She would never know unless she tried.

As the decision crystallized, she moved back to the kitchen. Picking up the cordless phone on the counter, she dialed Max's number and held her breath.

It rang a few times before she heard the click that someone had answered.

"Hello."

"Max?"

"Alexis?"

"Yes, it's me. I'm sorry to be calling so late."

"No, don't be." He really didn't sound as if he minded. It buoyed her confidence.

"I, uh . . . thought about it, and I would like to see

you again, but there's something you should know first."

His dark, sexy chuckle sounded in her ear. "I had a feeling there would be conditions."

"It's important to me to be honest."

"Well, how about you be honest over dinner tomorrow?"

Alexis's heart stopped. Dinner? Alone? With Max and her terrible secret? Her left hand flew into her hair, and she scrunched it. Suddenly she had a severe case of cold feet.

"Uh . . ."

"Is dinner too fast for you?" he teased.

"No, no," she made haste to reassure him. "I would love to have dinner with you."

A little too much to have the sense to refuse.

"Great. I'll pick you up at seven."

"How about we meet at seven at Crusades again?" she quickly suggested. She didn't want him to see her home and then jump to conclusions before she had a chance to explain her situation herself.

His voice sounded reluctant. "If that's what you'd prefer."

"Definitely."

"Okay, I'll give the concierge your name and make sure he knows to let you up."

"Perfect."

"I'm really looking forward to this, Alexis. I'm glad you rang."

Alexis hesitated before replying in kind. She wasn't

sure *she* was glad yet. She could just be setting herself up for one big fall. What if he didn't forgive her?

"I'll see you tomorrow, Max," she said instead.

"Yes, you will."

Max sat at the cozy table for two and drummed his fingers on the beautifully pressed white tablecloth. The brittle tension in his body was at odds with the drippy candlelight of his elegant surroundings.

Alexis was ten minutes late.

That didn't bode well for him. At this point, being stood up seemed like a realistic probability. She had sounded so nervous on the phone. As if she was on the verge of hanging up. Where was the confident femme fatale he had spoken with in his mother's library? How could he reassure her that it was safe to come back? Surely, whatever she had to tell him couldn't be that bad. Just as he finished the thought, she appeared, crossing the threshold with quiet grace.

Thank goodness.

He stood up. Their eyes met across the room as a hostess indicated the table where he was waiting. That one exchange was all it took. He almost lost his balance.

Yup! The chemistry was still there, more potent than last night, if that were possible. Dressed conservatively in fitted black pants and a sleeveless red evening top, Alexis wore her hair down and natural. A circumstance he had nothing to complain about. Too often women attempted elaborate hairstyles, cuts, and colors, aiming for sophistication and coming up with awkward. Alexis had a sexy earthiness about her that had drawn him right from the start. She didn't *try* to look great. She simply did.

"Hey." He smiled when she reached him.

"I hope you haven't been waiting long," she said as a waiter pulled out her chair.

"A few minutes," he lied, seating himself as she folded her body into the chair. The waiter handed them each a menu before departing.

"You look fabulous."

She grinned. "So do you."

He opened his menu. "I've started reading *Great Expectations.*"

"Really?" She raised her eyebrows. "And what do you think so far?"

"It's not as great as the title leads you to expect."

She laughed, and he loved the sound. When was the last time he'd had a simple, carefree moment like this one? With the media constantly invading every corner of his life, these moments were as rare as diamonds. The thought immediately reminded him of his dissatisfaction with his mother's security team.

"You're frowning." She recalled his attention.

"Am I?" He looked up in surprise. "Sorry. I didn't mean to be. Was just thinking about the run-in I had with our head of security this morning."

"Oh?"

"They didn't catch the intruder we had last night, and it's been bugging me all day."

"I see."

"It's ludicrous, you know," he told her. "After everything the media has put me and my family through, they still want more." He shrugged. "But it doesn't matter. I will find out who broke into my mother's house last night, and when I do, there will be hell to pay."

He nodded decisively. It was only a matter of time before his private investigator tracked the culprit down by using the cell phone she had stupidly left behind. Her anonymity would be short-lived, and so would her career. If there was anyone Max could enjoy taking down, it was a journalist. She would be punished.

"Hell to pay?" Alexis repeated faintly.

"They will never work in this town again, that's for sure."

He looked up to find Alexis studying him with worried concern. He immediately reached out to squeeze her hand. "I'm sorry, I shouldn't be burdening you with my problems. We came here to talk about you, so let's do that." He smiled. "So, what was it you wanted to tell me?"

Chapter Four

"May I take your order?"

Never had she been more grateful for the blunt interruption of an inconsiderate stranger. Alexis glanced up at the waiter and smiled graciously as her brain slipped into overdrive.

What? Tell him now, after the bomb he just dropped on me?

She couldn't. She needed time to think.

Was she doing the right thing? Or had she let her attraction to him get in the way of intelligent thought?

Ordering seemed like the perfect way to stall.

"Yes, I'd like to order," she announced, looking down at her menu, intending to order the first dish she saw. Unfortunately, it wasn't that simple.

Bollocks! It's in French. With irritation, she remembered the restaurant's speciality.

"Uh . . ."

"Would you like me to order?" Max asked gently.

She lifted her gaze from the menu to see his eyes twinkling at her. She blushed. "Yes."

"We'll have Chateaubriand *pour deux*." Max closed his menu and handed it back to the waiter. "It's a dish especially for couples," he said in a low voice across the table.

Alexis felt the warmth in her face spread through her bones.

"Very good, sir." The waiter inclined his head, re-filled their glasses, and departed.

So much for stalling.

Alexis shifted uncomfortably in her seat and then took a stab at the first safe topic she could think of.

"I guess living in Paris for a year must have taught you a few words."

"A few." Max smiled. "Enough to get by, and by that, I mean eat."

She forced a laugh. "The food in Paris is very good."

"Have you been to Paris?"

"Yes. The bakeries are the best. I loved their pastries." She didn't add that as a person on a backpacker's allowance, pastries were all she could afford. "Do you have a favorite restaurant there?" she asked instead.

A wry smile curled Max's handsome mouth as she posed the question. At first he didn't respond, just sat there looking at her over the rim of his wineglass as though trying to decipher an interesting puzzle. The effect on her senses was both frightening and seductive. She fiddled uneasily with the napkin in her lap.

"Alexis, is it just me, or are you deliberately changing the subject?"

She scanned his handsome face as he lowered his wineglass. A lock of brown hair fell across his forehead. Her fingers itched to push it off his face. It made him look vulnerable.

The one thing she knew he was not.

There was nothing vulnerable or endearing about the way he intended to punish the intruder who had broken into his mother's house on Saturday night.

His tone earlier had been without mercy—as if he was making a promise rather than a statement.

They will never work in this town again.

A chill ran down her spine. The threat could not help but make her pause. If she couldn't work, it was all over. She would lose the twins. Her brother-in-law was waiting in the wings. Not her sister's husband, but his brother—or should she say evil twin?—who watched her every move, waiting for a sign to stake his claim. The last time they had spoken, she had told him the job at *Starbuzz* was in the bag. At the time it had been true, but now . . . Now, not only had she sacrificed that opportunity, but she had no other prospects. Worse, Max was offering to fix it so she never would.

She couldn't let that happen.

Mel had chosen her to be the children's guardian. And she loved those kids more than she had ever thought she could. There was no way they were being shipped off to Adelaide. She wasn't ready to throw in the towel yet. Her fingers curled around the stem of her wineglass.

You've got to be strong.

Lifting her chin, she gave Max a look that was calculated to be both cheeky and flirtatious. She hid her emotions best behind a mask of allure.

"Do you always have to read an ulterior motive into everything I say and do?"

He raised his eyebrows. "Do I *always* do that?"

"Most certainly." She veiled her eyes. "You did it the last time we were here, and you're doing it now."

"The last time we were here?" he repeated.

"I said I had a headache, and you thought I was prevaricating."

"You *were*."

"Whether I was or I wasn't isn't the issue."

He laughed. "I see. Well, I guess I do tend to be a little suspicious when it comes to women. I'm sorry if I come across as too cynical."

Despite herself, she was curious. "Why are you suspicious of women?"

His expression turned pensive. He seemed reluctant to talk about it, confining his gaze to the wine he was swirling in his glass.

"It's nothing. Just a theory I had for a while." He spared her a brief smile that tugged at her heartstrings.

"What kind of theory?"

"Just the type of women I've dated in the past." His eyes met hers. "You're not an actor, are you?"

Depends on what you mean by actor.

Alexis hesitated. "No."

"I didn't think so." He grinned.

"What gives it away?"

"Well, for starters, I've never heard of you, and with your charisma, you'd be nothing less than A-list."

She choked, but his compliment touched her. "That's very flattering."

He shrugged. "It's the truth."

"So I take it your relationship with Julia Evans didn't go so well . . ."

" 'Relationship.' " He shook his head. "I wouldn't call it that. If anything, it was more like a business pro-posal. She thought dating me would further her career. Maybe I'd do a song for one of her movies. Maybe my fame would spark off hers and vice versa." His voice held a hint of self-mockery. "I might have gone with it if"—he hesitated—"if Kelly hadn't died." He paused a moment to ponder what he had just said. "That event kind of gave me a new perspective. A perspective Julia didn't really get."

She could see how that would happen. Success could get all-consuming, make you forget the important things in life until you were shocked into sitting up and taking notice. That's what had happened to Max.

"You know," he added thoughtfully, "you can really tell who your true friends are by the ones who stick around when you need them the most."

A shot of sympathy filtered through her body. How terrible to wake up one morning and realize that most of the people you knew really didn't care about you all that much and just wanted to use your fame and fortune for their own personal gain.

Like writing an article for Starbuzz Magazine *to earn money to support two kids.*

She inwardly cringed. How was she any better than all the actors and singers who had gone before her? No wonder he was so bitter.

"What about you?" he asked suddenly. "What was your last relationship like?"

The question seemed to come out of left field, and it made her pause, tilt her head, and think it over.

She'd been on a lot of dates, had the odd holiday fling in Europe, but those encounters had always been of a temporary nature. Before they started, they had an expiration date. The word *relationship* couldn't be applied to any of them.

She smiled cynically. "Oh, you don't want to know."

And maybe I don't want to tell you.

She couldn't imagine anything more humiliating than admitting she had never had a proper boyfriend. It wasn't because she hadn't been ready for something more serious. The right man had just never come along.

She had always envied her sister's certainty when she'd met the twins' father. Mel had known from the first he was The One. Their courtship had been short and intense. As an outsider looking in, she had seen how happy their marriage was. When the twins came, it had been like the icing on the cake.

She had always thought that one day she too would

get married and have children of her own. Never in her wildest dreams did she think that she would inherit her sister's kids. Not that she begrudged them her guardianship. She would do anything for those kids.

Anything.

"There is so much going on behind that smile, I'm afraid to ask," Max commented as their dinner arrived.

And she was too afraid to tell him. Last night, things had seemed so much simpler. She had thought all she would be sacrificing in telling him the truth was pride, but it looked as if she would be giving up her future income as well. She couldn't let that happen.

A silence fell between them. She didn't know what to say. Her food tasted like chalk. He wasn't going to forgive her easily. She had been a fool to come here tonight. Now she was stuck with the unhappy circumstance of having to figure her way out of it.

Max broke the silence. "I've been thinking a lot about what happened last night."

She swallowed. "With the intruder?"

"No." He frowned. "And I think I'm going to make that a closed topic for the rest of the evening."

The bitterness in his tone did nothing to reassure her.

"I was thinking about what happened in the library just before my security guard came in."

"Just before the . . ."

She felt fire light the base of her neck, and her face infused with heat as she remembered what they had been about to do just before Mr. Security had walked in.

"I asked you what you knew about music."

She let out a sigh of relief. "Oh, that . . ."

"Were you thinking of something else?" he drawled.

Again she felt her color rising.

"Don't worry, I thought about that too. Probably a lot more than you did. And I do intend—"

"Max," Alexis interrupted, grabbing her wineglass and taking a much needed gulp. "I don't know anything about music."

"Then you'll make the perfect muse. Of course," he added, "we'll have to spend a lot more time together, which may lead to—"

"About that," Alexis interrupted desperately again. It was time she nipped the whole affair in the bud before she chickened out. "You see," she began, "now that I have children, things like this are a little more complicated."

"And by that you mean . . ."

"I mean . . ." She swallowed. "I have to think about the children and how this will affect them."

"I understand completely. In fact—"

"Max," she cut him off. "I'm telling you this because the children are never far from my thoughts. Their future is . . ." She paused, trying to think of a strong enough word. "Paramount to me. Sometimes it has even affected my judgment in matters in which I shouldn't have let it."

"Okay, now you're losing me." Max reached across the table and took her hand, instantly suspending all thought as his fingers enveloped hers. "Family is very important to me too. You don't have anything to worry about on that score. I'm not the kind of guy who would do anything to hurt the twins. I get it—they've been through a rough time, losing their mother and father."

"Max, sometimes when people are desperate—"

Suddenly the waiter appeared again at Max's elbow, and she broke off.

"I'm sorry to interrupt, sir, but there is an urgent call for you. Do you wish to take it?"

Max looked up, frowning. "Who is it?"

"A gentleman by the name of Robert Hendricks."

"Robert," Max murmured. His gaze snapped back to Alexis, but this time it was apologetic. "I'm sorry, do you mind if I take this?"

Alexis shook her head. "That's fine. If you'll excuse me for a moment." They both stood up, and Alexis immediately darted off in the direction of the ladies' room, relieved at the prospect of a break to gather her flagging wits.

In the safety of the bathroom she dropped her handbag by the sink and leaned against the counter, examining her wan face in the mirror.

What are you doing?

Troubled brown eyes stared back at her, unable to answer the question. She was past stalling. Now she was just prolonging the agony of letting him go . . . again.

It was more difficult this time, because she had gotten to see more of him. More of the real Max behind that celebrity mask he wore.

But the fact was, he wore that mask to protect himself from people like her. Forgiveness was not going to come her way; he had certainly made that clear. She should have known that she was living in a fool's paradise. In fact, forgiveness was the least of her problems. She couldn't risk losing her reputation and a chance to get a proper job when her brother-in-law would jump at any excuse to take the twins from her. Her cards had completely changed, and her hand was not looking good.

She had to go back out there and cut the dinner short. Let Max down gently but firmly. Right now, no damage had been done, to either her income or his state of mind. She wanted to keep him in blissful ignorance. Let him have fond memories of her rather than bitter ones. The article would never be published anyway. He would never have to know as long as she ended it now.

Max watched the gentle sway of Alexis's graceful figure as she left their table. She was mesmerizing but so difficult to read. There was too much mystery behind her eyes, mystery and gentle regret. It was going to take a lot of charm to pull her out from behind the protective wall she had built around herself.

"Sir, would you come this way?"

Max tore his gaze from Alexis's hips and focused on the amused face of the waiter. "Sorry," he apologized, feeling the tips of his ears burn. "Lead the way."

The waiter led him to a private foyer near the entrance of the restaurant, where there was a phone sitting on the desk. The waiter pressed a few buttons and then handed the receiver to him.

"Robert?"

"Max, I'm sorry for interrupting your dinner. Do you want me to call back later?"

"No, no." Max took a deep breath. "I have to know. Did you manage to track down Saturday night's intruder?"

"Most definitely." He could hear the smile in Robert's voice. "She wasn't careful enough. We've got full identification—name, address, background information, criminal record, the works."

Max sighed with satisfaction and sank heavily into his chair. "Was I right?"

"I think so. It's not clear who she's working for exactly, but she has a degree in journalism. I would say she's freelancing."

At last, he had her where he wanted her.

In the palm of my hand.

Max's fingers curled into a fist on the desk. He would make an example of this brass-faced lowlife and at last show the media that he had not forgiven them for the death of his sister.

"When can we meet up to go through the details?" he asked his investigator.

"Well, unfortunately, I'm out of town for the next few days," Robert apologized, "but I'll be back Monday."

"Monday it is." Max nodded. "First thing."

Robert agreed, and they rang off.

Max went back to the table and sat down. He had waited only five minutes when he saw Alexis weaving through the tables toward him. She looked troubled and regretful. Not a good sign.

"Max." Her voice was husky when she reached him, and he noticed she did not sit down, so he stood up.

"What is it?"

"I've . . . I've just had a chance to think about this rationally, and it's not going to work out."

Dread tightened his throat. "What do you mean?"

"I mean us." She gestured between them. "It's just not right."

Max frowned. "What happened to change your mind?"

She shook her head. "I'm not ready, Max. I realize that now. I'm not ready for . . . for you. There is too much going on in my life right now. I have . . . I have a commitment to the children. They need me first."

It was the one thing he couldn't argue with. What was he supposed to say—stuff the children, and pick me? Of course she would put them first. The fact that she did only made his respect for her grow. When they first met, she had said she was afraid of being an adequate mother. She was already more of a mother than she knew.

She took a deep breath. "In fact, I think I should go."

"How about a dance?"

"I beg your pardon." Her expression was clearly frustrated. "Did you hear anything I just said?"

"I heard you." He smiled sadly. "And what's worse is, I understand. I just want one dance before you go. That's all I ask. And if you still want to leave, then I won't stop you." He indicated the sunken bar in the center of the room. A man was playing softly on the piano. There were a few couples on the small dance floor, swaying slowly to his gentle tune. Couples who were clearly in love, who existed only for each other in that soft, melodic moment.

Alexis looked at the scene uncertainly. He knew what she was thinking. That he just wanted an excuse to hold her. Well, so what? If this was good-bye, why not make it a good one?

She lifted her eyes to his, and he released a breath he hadn't realized he'd been holding. "Just one dance?"

"That's all."

"Okay."

He took her hand and led her to the floor. She turned easily into his arms, and it was sweet agony to hold her. She lay her cheek on his chest and sighed. His grip on her hand tightened as he rested his own cheek lightly on the top of her head. It was a moment in time. He could count every beat, feel every breath, every graze of skin. His senses were heightened beyond all reasonable levels. He didn't want to let her go.

With every moment that passed, he got a little more desperate. Did she feel how right they were together, how perfectly they fit? It was a tragedy to let this go.

He released her hand and lifted his own to her cheek, stroking its soft surface until she looked up.

"Alexis. Keep my number. When you're ready—"

She reached up and caught his hand. Turning her head, she pressed a quick kiss into his palm. "I'm sorry, Max. This is too hard. I really must go."

With deliberate slowness she pulled his hand away from her face and stepped out of his arms.

"Good-bye."

Max Deroux had never been so thoroughly rejected by a woman in his life, and he was still smarting from it when he sat down for breakfast with his mother at the end of week.

He didn't understand.

What had he done wrong? Somewhere between their dinner arriving and his phone call, something had happened to upset Alexis, and he had no means to contact her and ask her what it was. Should he run the risk of seeming like a stalker and ask his private investigator to track her down as well?

He groaned in frustration.

"You seem a little preoccupied this morning," his mother observed, handing him a pot of tea. "In fact, you've been out of sorts all week."

Max took the pot from her and poured himself a cup. "Sorry. I didn't mean to seem grumpy."

"You never do." Her lips twitched. "What's on your mind?"

He hesitated, wondering if there was any possibility of not telling her.

"Don't even think about it."

He grimaced. "It's a woman."

Ceilia opened her mouth and then shut it again. Slowly she picked up her fork and pierced a piece of egg, a smile curling her lips. *"Really."*

Max eyed her with reluctant amusement. "I wouldn't get too excited about it if I were you."

"Oh, Max! I knew you would meet someone. I knew—"

"Well, it's over."

"It hasn't begun!"

"*Because* she shot me down in flames," Max explained. "Made a run for it."

"Shot you down in flames!" Ceilia was clearly aghast. "But she couldn't have. It's not possible. I mean"—she threw up hands—"how could any woman not like you?"

She looked so incredulous that Max couldn't help but laugh. "You do wonders for my ego, Mum, but it really is quite conceivable that someone might find me and my life in the public eye somewhat less than attractive." He lifted the teapot and grimaced. Fame certainly hadn't done him any favors. He poured her some tea. "Drink your tea. It'll help calm your nerves."

Ceilia eyed her full cup contemptuously. "I am not drinking my tea until you've told me the whole story from start to finish."

"There's really not much to tell."

"Who is she?"

He shrugged. "Does it matter? I have no means of contacting her. She made sure of that. Besides"—he tried to make light of the matter—"I'm thinking about going back to Paris. Starting a new album."

He felt like writing again. Snatches of songs bubbled in his brain, and he wanted his piano so he could string a tune together.

"Hmm" was his mother's dubious response.

" 'Hmm,' what?"

"Since when are you interested in writing songs again? I thought all that was too 'empty' for you."

Alexis' words came back to him.

Singing is your life. Don't give it up because of some misplaced desire to punish yourself.

If nothing else, Alexis had certainly left him with a kick in the pants. That was the great thing about her: She always jumped to the heart of things. A gentle smile curved his lips, and his mother eyed it knowingly.

"She did this, didn't she? I want you to find this girl. I like her already."

Max sighed. "Mum, I told you. She rejected me."

"Try again. She wasn't in the right frame of mind."

"She was smart is what she was," he grunted as he drew the selection of magazines and papers the housekeeper had left for them toward him. A rueful grin twisted his mouth. "Too smart."

As he flicked through the magazines, one couldn't help but catch his eye. He was on the cover of it. Sure, the photo was old, but the headline was certainly new. *Max Deroux's Secret Pain.*

He ripped the magazine out of the stack, knowing instinctively that this was the work of Saturday night's intruder. Clearly the story was hot off the press. He wasn't too worried. After all, he'd left the party barely after getting there. But he was curious. What dirt did they think they had on him now?

"What is it?" His mother's voice broke in on his scattered thoughts. But he held up a hand for silence as he flipped through the magazine and began to read.

Max Deroux, jazz singer and international megastar, may never sing again. After a year-long self-inflicted exile in Paris, he finally decided to see his friends at his thirtieth birthday party last Saturday. It was apparent to onlookers that Max Deroux still suffered deeply from guilt, grief, and frustration over his sister's death on his Australian tour over a year ago.

Shortly after his appearance at the party, he took a friend aside and confessed that even his old flame Julia Evans could not lift his spirits. But depression isn't the only result of his sister's great tragedy. His career might be on the line as well.

"I wouldn't know what to sing about even if I could," he told his confidante. "Kelly was my muse. With her gone . . ."

Max Deroux dropped the magazine as if it had burned him.

No. This can't be happening.

He read the last line again. It was there in black and white. She had quoted him word for word. Either she had an extraordinary memory or she'd had a tape recorder. His mind reeled at the possibility.

This can't be!

Pride raged against the thought. Could he be such a fool?

Against his will, he bent his head to read more.

The loss of a loved one is always hard, but when you blame yourself, it's even worse. Max Deroux not only believes that it is his fault his sister died but that he should be punished for it. It is this guilt that renders the poor man incapable of pursuing his career further. It is clear that he withdrew from society not simply to mourn but to deal with this secret pain.

"Do you honestly think if I hadn't been so caught up with my fans and my singing and all that nonsense that my sister wouldn't still be alive today?" and "I let all that fame crap get to me. I let it rule my life. I should have been more vigilant. I should have paid more attention."

Max had seen enough. Anger raced through his body and left him trembling. Noise cluttered his head. Threads of their conversation came back to him. Different scenes raced through his mind, each one strangling him with its lies. Her sweet smile, the mystery in her eyes, that seductive sweep of her eyebrow.

That witch!

Could he have been a bigger idiot? He had fallen for her charade, hook, line, and sinker. Worse, he had wanted more. Since when did he fall for a good pair of legs and a twinkle in the eye? He prided himself on being smarter than that. He had vowed that he would never get drawn in by the media again. Never be manipulated and hung up in their devious plots. And yet here he was, the vow still whispering off his lips, and he was in their hands again. He couldn't decide whom he was more furious at, himself or her.

Oh, no, definitely her.

To think . . . He shuddered. He had asked that snake out on date, for Pete's sake. The enormity of his delusion struck him like a lightning bolt. What a complete and utter fool she had made of him and his grief.

Were there no standards in this world anymore?

"Max."

He felt a hand on his arm, and he turned maddened eyes to his mother, who immediately snatched her hand away under his stinging glare.

The sweetheart of jazz had only one thought tearing through his body.

Revenge.

Ever since Alexis had decided that *Starbuzz Magazine* was where she wanted to work, she had taken out a subscription so she could keep tabs on the kind of stories they published. As a result, *Max Deroux's Secret Pain* landed in her mailbox hot off the presses on Friday. However, not realizing there was anything urgently requiring her attention in the issue, she had held off reading it until she had some free time on Monday morning. It was 8:30 A.M., just after breakfast, and the twins were still in bed. They had kept her up most of the night with nightmares about the accident again. It seemed to plague Kayla more than Holly. In any event, the girls hadn't fallen back to sleep till about three in the morning, leaving Alexis hoping they would sleep late. At least then she would have a chance to catch up on her mail and job hunting.

Sitting down at the kitchen table, she pulled *Starbuzz* from its plastic envelope. She stared in stunned horror at the headline and then tore the magazine open to the story in question.

It was like being doused with cold water. She could not take her eyes from the words on the page. She stared at them for so long, they began to blur. And then her stomach lurched.

Oh, God!

She was going to be sick. Her chair scraped back violently on the wooden floor, and she flew from the dining room. She skidded into the bathroom, sank to her knees in front of the toilet, and threw up.

It took her a while to calm down. Her brain and stomach were somersaulting at the same time, making her dizzy.

How could this happen?

Finally she took a deep breath and stood up, wiping a shaky hand over her mouth. She knew how it had happened. Sandra had to be behind this. She recognized the writing style, and Sandra was the only person she had told. It couldn't be anyone else.

She glanced at her reflection in the mirror and was immediately repulsed. Her face was a pasty white, her lips, bloodless. She turned on the tap and washed her hands and then her face with warm water. It seemed to help, though not much.

What am I supposed to do now?

But even as she asked herself the question, she realized that there was nothing she could do. The story was out. The interview was in print. She couldn't erase the words from people's memories. The damage was irrevocably done. It was too late.

She grabbed her toothbrush and vigorously brushed her teeth. She hated being so powerless. Feeling so used. After running a comb through her hair, she tied the sash of her red satin dressing gown more securely around her waist. There was no use feeling sorry for herself. Especially considering the offense to her was minor when compared to poor Max.

Poor Max!

How much betrayal could one person take?

She could only imagine how he would feel when he saw the article.

How he would . . .

Her heart stopped.

He would think she was behind it all. Again her stomach lurched, even though there was nothing left in it.

Will he come after me?

Wringing her hands, she left the bathroom and poked her head into the twins' bedroom. They were both still dead to the world, their cherub faces so peaceful, so trusting. They thought they were safe, so ignorant were they of her inner turmoil.

It was then that the events of that fateful night came back to her. She had been with the twins when Sandra let herself out. The woman must have used the opportunity to steal the broken tape, and somehow she had repaired it.

Again her eyes fell to the sleeping girls. How could she protect them if Max wouldn't let his vendetta go? She swallowed. Max had no way of knowing it was Sandra, not she, who had written the article. Man! When she got her hands on Sandra, that girl was going to get a dressing-down she'd never forget. She never should have approached Sandra for help. But you live, you learn.

Boy, do you learn.

Alexis left the bedroom, closing the door softly behind her.

What could she do? What could she do?

She raced back into the living room. Grabbing her purse, she rummaged through it until she found the card Max had given her. Marching into the kitchen, she took the phone off the receiver and punched in the number.

The least she could do was apologize, try to explain, try to help. If she could . . .

The phone rang twice before someone picked it up.

"Max speaking."

"Max," she rushed out, "it's me, Alexis."

"How fitting that you should call me now."

"What . . . what do you mean?" she stammered.

"I'm here, Alexis."

She heard the dial tone and then a knock at the door. It took her a full three seconds to realize what was going on. Slowly she replaced the receiver.

He's here?

The knocking grew louder as she stood there staring at the door in shock. The knocking soon became pounding, which finally broke her trance. She hurried forward, yanking the door open.

"Hey! There's no need to—"

The words died on her lips as a large masculine figure filled the threshold. A figure she thought she'd never see again. A figure radiating rage, revenge, and raw masculinity.

Chapter Five

I am so dead.

Her fingers froze on the doorknob as she stared at Max. He didn't wait to be invited in but simply walked right past her. She was left with nothing to do but close the door. After a moment's pause, she did so. The resounding click as it slipped into its frame couldn't help but intone the finality of her fate. She turned, bracing herself against the flat plane of the door. Her fingers curled behind her back as she leaned against the dark wood.

"Clearly you weren't expecting me." His thunderous gaze raked her from head to foot. "Though I can't imagine why."

Alexis felt her cheeks burn red as she remembered what she was wearing. She jerked the flaps of her red satin robe together, hiding the matching slip beneath.

86

"Of course I wasn't expecting you." She tied the sash with a defiant twist. "I thought I'd never see you again."

"Did your research teach you so little about me?" His voice was pure contempt.

She lifted her chin. "How did you find me?"

"My private investigator had your cell phone. It wasn't hard to get an address."

She could have kicked herself.

Of course.

How could she have been so stupid? Those things were traceable. Even if the article hadn't come out, he would have found her anyway. The absolute futility of her situation sank in, and she felt cold all over.

"You made it easy," he began. "But even if you hadn't, did you honestly think I would just let you get away with it? Just let it go? Just like that?"

She blanched under his accusing stare, guilt and mortification coursing through her veins. She hadn't thought that. She had hoped it.

Prayed it.

Talk about wishful thinking.

The fact was, he deserved an explanation. She owed him that much. It was the least she could do after the mess she'd made of everything. But where to start? She tried to think of a coherent opening but ended by saying the first dumb thing that came into her head. "I guess you've read the article."

"You guess!" he exploded. "The whole world's read that article, Alexis. Not just me." He stopped, shaking his head in amazement as he seemed to realize something.

All she could do was watch him in agonized suspense. "How many lies have you told?" he ground out. "How many laws have you broken to get this story? Have you no shame?"

"I am *very* ashamed of my part in all this." She ran agitated fingers through her hair. "But, Max, you've got to know how sorry I am. I lost control of the situation. I never meant for that article to be published."

"Oh, so you just crashed my birthday party by accident," he retorted. "What do you think I am, stupid?"

"No, I—"

"You planned this. Meticulously planned it and carried it out. You knew exactly what you were doing. And for what?"

"The children I told you, my sister—"

"No more lies!" he silenced her. "I might have believed that last week. But I'm not going to be drawn in by your sob stories again."

"But—"

"Oh, I know you're good." His eyes raked her body again, and she wished that she wasn't quite so exposed. "You must be the best in the business. Such a great asset to that magazine, willing to lie, cheat, and even seduce in the name of profits."

She gasped. "I never seduced you."

"Oh, come on, Alexis, we both know what you were doing the night of my party! You would've done anything to get me to talk about my sister's death."

Okay, maybe she had been a little flirtatious. Perhaps trailing your fingers across a pair of manly shoulders *was* called seduction these days. That hadn't been any-thing to do with getting him to talk. It had more to do with the fact that he was so good-looking and it was an effort to keep her hands to herself. Even now, his blue eyes flashing as if he literally wanted to grab her by the throat and choke the life out of her only made her want to reach out and brush the stray lock of hair off his forehead.

She put a hand to her temple. "I must be going mad."

"You're not seriously claiming insanity, are you?"

Her eyes flew to his, realizing she must have spoken that last thought out loud. He glared back at her without even blinking, and she knew she had to explain herself.

"You're right." She squared her shoulders. "I did come to your birthday ball for a story, and, yes, I did record our conversation on tape. But I swear to you, as soon as I got home, I destroyed the tape."

"Well, you know what?" Max folded his arms, every line in his body radiating disdain. "I might be tempted to believe you *if* everything I said wasn't published *word for word in a gossip magazine.*"

"Max, I honestly—"

"Don't *ever* use that word with me. You don't know the meaning of it. Tell me," he added sarcastically, "did you want to see me again at Crusades because you thought you might have missed part of the story?"

"No! I wanted to see you again because I wanted to confess everything."

"How telling that you didn't!"

"Max, please—"

"I trusted you." His voice was raw with emotion. "I thought you were different. I thought . . ." He looked heavenward and then back at her, hurt and pain marring his perfect features. "I thought we understood each other. When we talked—" He broke off, stuffing his hands into the pockets of his trousers and looking at the ground in confusion.

She knew exactly how he felt, because she had felt it too. That night, their first date, this morning, this minute. They felt connected. And in ways she had never felt connected with anyone else.

He looked up. "How much are you getting for it, anyway?"

"For what?"

"The article! Damn it!"

"Nothing, I swear. I didn't write it."

But he wasn't listening.

"Fifty thousand? Maybe sixty? Certainly enough to get you out of here." He looked around at her house, and then his gaze returned to hers. "Is that why you pretended you knew my sister, Alexis? Why you had the audacity to use a person who is deceased to get to me?"

She moved away from the door. "I didn't—"

He took a menacing step closer. "Yes, you did." And then his voice lowered till it was unnaturally calm. "You know you did."

He was right. Letting him jump to his own conclusions and not correcting him was just as bad. She bit her tongue as his eyes raked her body with scorn.

"Do you know how low that is? Do you?"

She put a hand to her throat, and it constricted beneath her palm. What was it about guilt that made you so sick, you couldn't speak?

"After Kelly died, I vowed that this would never happen again," Max continued without mercy. "That I would never be manipulated by the media again. I can't let it go, Alexis." His eyes locked with hers. "I won't."

Finally she knew that her worst fears were about to be realized. He was going to make her pay and pay in full, at the cost of her sister's children and her own dignity. "Revenge will not make you feel any better, Max," she choked. "Please—"

"Who said anything about revenge?" His eyes sparkled with a light she did not trust. He walked toward her, every stride predatory, muscles flexing under the thin fabric of his white shirt. "I'm going to give you exactly what you want, exactly what you came to me for in the first place."

She gasped as he grabbed her arm and tugged her back toward the door.

"Max, what are you—"

He flung the door open and pulled her out onto the shabby old porch. That's when she saw the reporters accompanied by their cameramen milling about on her front lawn. The photos started almost the second the old boards creaked under their feet. She tried to turn away from the bright lights, but Max took advantage of her confusion by drawing her effortlessly into his arms.

Chest to chest.

Hip to hip.

Thigh to thigh.

Her skin sizzled in shock. She arched back over his arm, looking up into his face. "What are you doing?"

"You wanted to know what my life was like," he hissed. "And now you shall."

It was only then that the realization sank in—the enormity of what was about to happen. She should have pushed him away. She should have screamed, done something—anything. But the second his lips touched hers, she was lost.

It was like being caught in a riptide. She was simply swept away and powerless to stop it. He kissed her like a man possessed with rough, hungry passion. He wanted to punish her, and yet . . .

She reached up, pushing her fingers into his hair, cradling his head in her hands.

"I'm . . . so . . . sorry," she rasped against his mouth. He lifted his head at that, and she saw the pain, immense and naked, reflected there in his cobalt blue eyes. "You don't deserve this," she whispered.

It seemed as if time stood still. She heard the cameras clicking in the background, but the noise faded into static. The flurry of reporters around them blurred out of focus. It was just the two of them. A man and a woman, trying to deal with the giant rift between them.

"Damn you, Alexis Banks," Max swore hoarsely, and his lips fell to hers again.

Differently this time.

Gentle. Uncertain. Tender. They trembled over hers, coaxing a response, which she gave.

It was madness.

He had come for retribution, not to surrender his soul. The thought seared through his body, demanding attention. He tore his mouth from hers.

What am I doing?

He scanned her face. Tumultuous eyes, swollen lips, vulnerability in the very set of her jaw. How could such a beautiful face house such deceit? Her dark hair was splayed across her shoulders in tousled disarray. He wanted to run his fingers through it but dared not. Who knew where that would lead? It wasn't fair. Why did it have to be her?

Alexis Banks.

The woman who had humiliated him, tricked him, and lied to him.

It was the reporters who recalled his attention.

"Max, is Alexis Banks your Blue Angel?"

"Is it true you were together at Crusades on Sunday?"

"How long have you been seeing each other?"

Utterly caught up in the moment, he had completely forgotten about the journalists—the demons he had summoned there himself. They were edging closer, determination in their faces. Why didn't he just go, as he had planned? He had finished what he had come here to do. It was time to let the reporters show Alexis the error of her ways. And yet . . . he couldn't.

Abruptly, Alexis pushed away from him, and he let her go without resistance. She backed away from him toward the door as the reporters surrounded the porch.

Two small figures were standing in the doorway. Two little girls, dressed in pajamas. They raced up behind Alexis and clutched at her deliciously bare legs.

"Auntie Alex, what's going on?"

"Auntie Alex, who is that man you were kissing?"

It was like being punched in the gut. Max felt hot and then cold as he took in the cherub faces, the white blond curls, the aquamarine eyes. His mind reeled. Of all the things not to lie about, it had to be that.

What have I done?

But the reporters were getting braver; a couple of them had mounted the steps.

"Alexis, is it true that you and Max only met at his birthday ball?"

"Alexis, are you pregnant with his child?"

"Is your relationship with Max Deroux set for marriage?"

He watched as Alexis quickly gathered her girls to her, holding them protectively by her side. Max's lips tightened.

Why am I feeling sorry for her? She's one of them!

But as one of the journalists stepped up onto the porch, Max stood in front of him, shielding Alexis and the twins with his body. "Stop." He put a hand up.

The journalist immediately thrust a microphone under Max's mouth. "Are you in love with her, Max?"

Max glanced over his shoulder at Alexis. "Go inside and lock the door."

He saw her hesitate, and his heart writhed in his chest. She didn't know whether to trust him, but she didn't know what else to do.

He turned around. "Go!"

She looked down at the children. "Come on, girls." And the three of them backed into the house. He did not turn around until the door was safely closed behind them.

It was stupid. It really was.

He had come here to teach her a lesson, and yet there he was, taking her punishment.

Alexis sagged against the door.

She deserved this.

She had, after all, intended to write the article. The fact that she had changed her mind and Sandra had stolen her work was only a small consolation. If only he had given her a chance to explain properly.

Idiot!

She might have started out on the wrong side of the fence, but she had been securely on his side for days. This was Sandra's deceit, not hers. And the twins! They were blameless. Why should they pay?

Anger pushed her guilt aside.

She went to the window and gently parted a section of the blinds so she could peep out. They were still there. And he was standing on her porch answering all their questions. Pity she couldn't make out what he was saying. Probably sinking her further and further into his little payback scheme. She shuddered as a new fear gripped her. Would she ever be able to leave her house again? Those journalists couldn't possibly camp outside her house all day, could they? Alexis thought of Sandra.

Oh, yes, they could.

"Auntie Alex, why did you kiss that man?"

Her hand immediately dropped from the blinds, and she looked down. Two pairs of blue eyes stared up at her.

Perfect.

She didn't know which was worse, the interrogators outside or in. How was she going to explain this to the twins?

"Sometimes . . ."—she rolled the word off her tongue—"when you're not paying attention . . . things just happen." She walked away from the window toward the kitchen, and the girls followed her.

"Is he your boyfriend?"

She spun around. "No!" When their little faces grew fearful, she inwardly cursed her temper and repeated herself, softly this time. "No, my darlings."

She bit her lip, dragging a hand through her tangled hair. Hair that he had thrust his fingers into only moments before. Ruthless he was, but, boy, he was some kisser.

So many different emotions collided in her head, making her heartbeat slow and then fast by turns. Shame, excitement, anger, arousal. No two thoughts were alike. She wanted to kill and kiss him. Slap him and beg his forgiveness.

Arrogant, stubborn fool. Why didn't he just let me speak? Explain myself!

"Auntie Alex, are we in trouble?" The small, anxious voice below immediately made her heart melt. Her first priority had to be the twins. She put her hand on Holly's small shoulder and then sank to her knees.

"No, love. You're not in trouble."

She looked over their pajamas and forced a smile. "How about we get you two bathed and dressed?" She took them both by the hand and led them to the bathroom. She knelt beside the bath and began to fill it.

As she put her hand under the tap to test the water, worry seated itself firmly on her chest. If she couldn't leave this house, how was she supposed to get a job? How was she supposed to support the twins? How was she supposed to make her case to their uncle?

She turned off the water and helped the girls undress. She needed to get a job, a good job, if she was to raise the twins in the manner her sister would have wanted. There were so many things they needed or would need in the future. A good school, health insurance, a safe and comfortable home they could be proud of. Her Social Security allowance didn't stretch very far. And the first person to tell her all that would be her-brother-in-law, Paul Grant. This was his chance. He had been eyeing her situation with growing anticipation for the last month and constantly comparing it to his more "stable" circumstances.

She had promised him she was getting a job at *Starbuzz Magazine.* But that was definitely no longer in the cards. He would be on her case again soon. She knew he was just biding his time.

Waiting for her weakest moment.

Her heart quaked. She couldn't lose the twins. Not when her sister had specifically requested that she be their guardian. She couldn't let Mel down, not when she knew why Mel had wanted her over Paul and Lisa.

An hour and no answers later, the girls were clean and dressed.

She went back to the window, and it was with great relief that she saw that her front yard was empty. Max must have somehow gotten rid of them. She opened the front door and stepped onto the porch to be sure. Immediately a hidden flash blinded her, and she retreated inside and closed the door. So, they were still out there, just being more discreet about it.

Suddenly the phone rang.

"Hello?"

"Hello, is this Alexis Banks?"

"Yes."

"I'm Lisa Marks, from Channel Eight. I'd just like to get a statement regarding your relationship with Max Deroux."

Alexis pulled the phone away from her ear and looked at it in disgust. How on earth had they gotten her number so fast?

"There is no relationship between me and Max Deroux."

"Ms. Banks, you were seen with Mr. Deroux at Crusades last week. You were also seen this morning at your house, locked in what witnesses say was a passionate embrace. Are you pregnant with his child?"

Alexis put the phone down as if it were a poisonous snake and just sat there staring at it for a moment. She shook her head.

Who are these people?

Squaring her shoulders, she glanced at the twins to make sure they were okay. They were both engrossed in a television show, seemingly oblivious to all that was going on around them. Thank goodness for small mercies.

The phone rang again. With a sigh she picked it up. "Hello?"

"Hi, Alexis, I'm Greg from *ABN News.* How long have you and Max Deroux been seeing each other?"

"We're not seeing each other!" Alex cried, and then she quickly softened her voice as Holly looked up. She turned her body into the counter, away from prying little-girl eyes. "Where did you get this number?"

But the reporter ignored her.

"Why are you and Max keeping this affair a secret?"

"I—" Alex fumed. "We're not keeping it a secret. There is no affair."

Again she slammed the phone down.

Ugh! She stared at the phone, just daring it to ring again. She shouldn't have cast out the challenge, because it did. This time, however, she was ready. She snatched up the receiver.

"I am not answering any questions. I am not dating Max Deroux. And I want you to tell everyone in your industry to leave me and my family alone or I'm taking out a restraining order against all of you!"

"It's okay. It's me."

The second she heard his thick, velvety voice, the muscles in her chest tightened. There was a reason he was such a great singer. His voice strummed her nerves like guitar strings. It took away her breath and made her heart leap. She leaned heavily against the counter.

"Max?"

He immediately heard the tension in her voice and knew the reason for it. There was still so much hanging in the air between them. That kiss was still too close. His grip on the receiver tightened. Before he thought, he asked the first thing that came into his head.

"Are you okay?"

"Yes." She hesitated. "I mean, no. I mean—" She stopped talking abruptly, and then her tone completely changed. "What do you care, anyway? You planned the whole underhanded event."

True. He had been asking himself the same question all the way home and then for half an hour in his mother's study before calling her.

Why did he care?

She was a reporter, the embodiment of everything he hated, the same breed of evil that had killed his sister. She had tricked him and lied to him. He had given her exactly what she deserved and in exactly the manner he had planned. And yet . . . He rubbed his temple.

"There were a few things I didn't count on."

"Like what?"

The vulnerable look in your eyes.

The taste of your lips on mine.

The way you ignored the reporters just to say sorry to me.

His fingers curled into fists as he cut off his wayward thoughts.

"You've got children," he said out loud. It was true, after all. He never would have done what he did if he had known it would involve the kids.

"What's that got to do with anything?"

"Come on, Alexis. Credit me with a little decency. I never would have intentionally dragged them into this. If I'd known—"

"But you did know," she accused. "I told you about Holly and Kayla the night I met you."

Latent anger boiled up again, and he had to fight the urge to slam his hand down on his mother's desk. "How was I supposed to know what was true and what was false? I still don't know."

Was that kiss an act?

Or did you feel something for me like I felt for you?

"Do you have any idea what you've done?" Her hoarse demand jolted him back.

"Yes, I do. And for the children's sake, I am sorry. This afternoon I tried to get them to believe we are not having an affair, but after that kiss . . ." He found he couldn't continue, and she didn't help him out by filling in the blanks, so he cut to the chase. "To cut a long story short, they now believe we're trying to have a secret affair."

"Why would we keep it a secret?"

An alarming thought occurred to him as he realized he really didn't know much about this woman. In his haste to see her, he hadn't read through the file his private investigator had given him. Abruptly he remembered how she had skirted his questions at Crusades. He walked around the desk and sank heavily into a chair behind it.

"Maybe . . . Maybe you're already in a relationship. Are you married? Do you have a boyfriend?"

"No."

Her answer held no hesitation, and, despite himself, he couldn't help the relief he felt.

"Max, how can we make this right?"

Her soft question was like a caress, but it immediately put him on defense. He had to remember how good she was. This woman was a journalist, for crying out loud, a professional manipulator. She could probably wriggle a confession out of the Pope if she wanted to. Physical attraction was a red herring, and he would do better to ignore it.

"Look," he returned matter-of-factly, "I feel bad about the children."

"Just the children?"

He ignored her comment. "I'm sending a guy over. He's a bodyguard."

"A bodyguard?" Her voice was confused.

"To keep you and the girls safe."

"I don't want a bodyguard," she retorted. "I want to explain to you what happened that night, and I want my life to go back to normal."

"I'm afraid that can't happen."

"Which one?"

"Both."

There was a weighted pause, and he knew he had rankled her. Finally! Evidence she wasn't completely infallible.

"You are so stubborn." Her voice was heavy with frustration.

"Because I've taken offense at what you did?" he scoffed.

"Max, I didn't write that article. It was a friend of mine who was over here the night of your party. She stole the tape."

"I thought you said you destroyed the tape."

"I did, but—"

"I don't know, Alexis. Your story keeps changing. A little too convenient, if you ask me."

"Max, punishing me is not going to somehow make up for what happened to your sister . . ."

He closed his eyes as if it could shut out her words. "I didn't call you to hear more of your excuses or your lame attempts at psychology. I called to offer you a bodyguard."

"So I'm confined to house arrest?"

"No, you'll be able to go out. You'll just need to take John or Tony with you."

Alexis's laugh was brittle. "What about work? How am I supposed to earn a living with a bodyguard in tow?"

He paused, thinking bitterly about her job at *Starbuzz Magazine.* So much the better if she couldn't go back.

"The money you earned from the last article you wrote should tide you over for a while."

"I told you, I didn't write it."

"Look, I'm not talking in circles with you. A body-guard will be there first thing in the morning, and that's final."

"Do you honestly think that's going to fix every-thing? There are things you don't know, other factors at stake. My brother-in-law—"

"If you have family problems, deal with them in your normal manipulative way. I'm sure you'll be fine."

Her voice was hoarse with emotion, and he had to clench the phone under its intensity. "For goodness' sake, Max, I'm not that kind of person, and if you had taken the time—no, *bothered* to hear my side of the story—then maybe you would have figured that out by now. I am as much a victim here as you are, and—"

He hung up, put his cell on the desk in front of him and sat staring at it for what seemed like an inter-minable period.

Man, she was good.

If she got any more convincing, he might just believe her, and he couldn't afford to do that.

The dial tone sounded painfully in Alexis's ear, and she slammed the phone down. Curse the man! He had done it again. She thought back to their date at Crusades with a cynical smile. He had been so ready to make a re-lationship work between them at any cost. It was hard to believe that the same man now wanted the complete opposite. The thought caused "what ifs" to trouble her for the rest of the day.

Her mood did not improve when that night she received a call from another man who was equally incensed.

"Paul," Alexis sighed into the receiver. "How did I know it would be you?"

"This is not a joke, Alexis." Her brother-in-law's voice was stern and cold. "I just saw you on the news in your underwear."

Alexis frowned. "I wasn't in my *underwear.*"

"Well, you might as well have been. Not to mention the wanton way you kissed that scandalous singer on your front porch like a regular tramp."

"How dare you!"

But Paul hadn't finished. "Do think this is the type of environment my brother would have wanted his children raised in?"

"It was a kiss, Paul," Alexis said through clenched teeth. "One kiss, which I have no intention of repeating anyway."

"For now," Paul scoffed. "But you're young and reckless. You won't be able to control yourself."

"You're overreacting."

He sighed as one trying to draw patience from an empty source. "The twins have just lost their parents, and their grandparents died before they even knew them. They need a stable environment. You can't be introducing your passing flings to them left, right, and center. What if they got attached to one of them?"

"I assure you," Alexis returned firmly, "the needs of the twins are my top priority."

"Chasing after high-profile singers seems to be higher on your list," Paul snorted. "Those types are fickle, Alexis. He'll be no good for the twins."

"Max has had nothing to do with the twins. We aren't seeing each other. It's over."

"So he was a one-night stand," Paul returned sarcastically. "Even better."

Alexis groaned in frustration. "It wasn't a one-night stand!"

"Then what was it, Alexis?" His voice was sharp and merciless. "Because I'm just dying to know."

"It was . . ." Alexis clenched the phone, feeling as if she was being helplessly backed into a corner. "It was a misunderstanding, that's what it was."

Her brother-in-law choked. She didn't blame him. Even to her own ears her explanation sounded lame. She and Max had kissed on that porch like there was no tomorrow, and if Paul had seen even half of what she'd felt in that instant, there was no way he was buying a word she said, even if it was true. He proved her point with his next sentence.

"Do you think I'm an idiot?"

"If you'd just let me tell you the full story."

"There's only one thing I want to know from you," Paul informed her. "Did you get that job you promised me was in the bag?"

His second attack, while not unexpected, caught her off guard by its abruptness.

"Uh . . ."

"Did you get that job at the magazine or not?"

"Well . . ."

"You didn't, did you?"

"Well, no. But there's no need to worry, because I have heaps of other opportunities that I'm about to—"

"Alexis." Paul let out a deep, thwarted sigh. "I've heard all this before. Again and again and again. I can't trust you."

Alexis felt her panic rising. "Yes, you can. I'll try harder. I'll—"

"I've spoken about this with my wife."

Of course you have.

"We both agree."

Of course you do.

"You're not a fit parent for those kids, and we're suing for custody. We deserve those children."

Alexis felt the ground give way under her feet as her worst nightmare started to take shape.

"They are not a prize to be won, Paul."

"There is no doubt that this situation is unfortunate. But you can't argue that Lisa won't make a great mother. Perhaps even better than the one they lost."

Bile rose in her throat, and her voice trembled as she spoke. "Mel was a fantastic mother! The best anyone could ever have, and she trusted me, not you or Lisa, to—"

He cut her off. "Mel couldn't have known that this would happen so soon. For goodness' sake, you're twenty-four years old, Alexis, freshly home from Amsterdam—"

Alexis felt like pulling out her hair. "What's Amsterdam got to do with anything?"

"You're young, wild, and careless. And most of all, you're not ready. Not like we are."

"I am ready."

"I'm sorry, Alexis, but this latest business with Max Deroux has made up my mind. You've had your chance. We'll take it from here."

It was the second time that day that Alexis heard the dial tone sounding loudly in her ear. This time, however, she was too poleaxed to slam down the receiver. She stared at it in disbelief until one of the twins recalled her attention by tugging on her sleeve.

"Auntie Alex, what's Haam-sster-dam?"

The innocent words tore at her heart as she blinked back tears. "It's a place."

"Is that where hamsters come from?"

"No, darling."

"Auntie Alex, can we get a hamster?"

"I don't know." She bit her lip, feeling her world crumbling around her. "Can we talk about it in the morning? It's time for you and your sister to go to bed."

Mel, how could you have thought I could do this?

Unbidden, Max's face seemed to materialize before her eyes, his raw faith in her simmering in his smile.

You can do this.

She took Kayla's hand.

Not if Paul had anything to say about it.

Chapter Six

True to his word, Max's bodyguard showed up at about seven the following morning and, despite Alexis's protests, stationed himself on the front porch. He remained there in a distinctly stubborn fashion until late evening. At that point he was replaced by another man, the "night shift," whom Alexis had a sneaky suspicion she had seen before. Possibly on the back door of Ceilia Deroux's mansion not so long ago.

In any case, neither of them was very accommodating when it came to her wishes. As far as they were concerned, they had their orders, and anything she had to say was irrelevant. And even when she demanded to be allowed to take it up with Max instead, they refused to give her his contact details. In her book, this was by far the most frustrating of their actions.

The problem with wanting to talk to a megastar when

he had disconnected the phone number he had originally given you, was that you couldn't just phone the operator to ask for his new one. Max Deroux, Alexis soon found out, wasn't a person, he was an institution. An institution that was surrounded by a very thick, very rude layer of public relations and security personnel who wouldn't give her his number if she was the last source of food on earth. Short of breaking into his mother's home again, she had no means to contact him. It was up to him to contact her, and she was pretty certain of the probability of that happening.

Zero.

As for her fellow journalists, they didn't *stop* calling her. Did they honestly think that hassling her every second was somehow going to change her mind about an interview? How was she supposed to make Paul believe that there was nothing going on between her and Max if the rest of the world insisted that there was?

She had never felt so thwarted in her life. She was completely at the mercy of her environment and had no power whatsoever to change or influence it. Her sister's children were going to be taken from her if she didn't find a way to A) Get a job and B) Get Max and his scandals out of her life.

Getting a job was actually proving to be the tougher problem. Her training was in journalism, but there wasn't one magazine, newspaper, or television station that would let her sign up without the proviso that she give them exclusive rights to her "story." A story that didn't even exist and her conscience wouldn't allow her to make up.

The only person who could set them right was shutting her out. And she didn't know what made her more angry—the fact that he was ignoring her or that he did it so effortlessly.

Two days passed, and still Max remained silent. She sent messages to him through the bodyguards, demanding that he call her, saying that they needed to talk. He ignored all her messages.

On the third day, a letter from Paul's lawyer arrived.

Attention: Ms. Alexis Banks

Dear Madam:

We act for Paul and Lisa Grant ("the Grants"). Please find enclosed by way of service a Notice of Motion we have filed with the Guardianship and Administration Board on behalf of the Grants.

The Notice of Motion challenges your custody of Holly and Kayla Grant ("the Children") on the basis that you are unfit to be their guardian because:

1. You are unemployed and financially insecure;
2. You cannot provide adequate living conditions for the Children; and
3. You are mentally and emotional unsound and not a fit and proper person to care for any child.

We kindly request you notify us within two weeks of the date of this letter that you concede custody of the Children to the Grants. If you do consent to giving custody of the Children to the Grants, we will proceed this matter to a court hearing and seek the Grants' legal expenses from you by way of a costs order.

We await your reply.

> *Yours faithfully,*
> *Geoff Rushby*
> *Partner*
> *Renfrey Dawson,*
> *Barristers & Solicitors*

enc.

It was the last kick in a long line of assaults. It also put a time limit on her need to get her life together.

She had two weeks.

Two weeks to prove to Paul that his three accusations were wrong. Max was the key. She really had to talk to him now, and, considering that he wasn't responding to messages, perhaps a trip back to the Deroux mansion was in order. This time, however, she'd do it with dignity by the light of day.

And she'd knock first.

That very afternoon, she arranged for a babysitter to come over and look after the twins. Then she asked her bodyguard to drive her to Ceilia Deroux's mansion. He was reluctant at first. But when she explained to him that if he didn't take her, he'd just be following her taxi, he had to concede to her stubbornness.

It wasn't a long drive to the Deroux mansion, and by the time they got there, Alexis was hyped and ready.

The entrance to the estate consisted of a short driveway leading up to a black iron gate flanked on both sides by the high masonry wall Alexis had climbed over the last time she was there. It looked even more intimidating in daylight. The bodyguard pulled up the car by the intercom on one side and wound down his window.

He pressed the doorbell and was responded to by security on the inside.

"Tony?" the gate operator responded. "Is that you? What are you doing here?"

Tony flicked an irritated glance in Alexis's direction before replying. "I've got Alexis Banks with me, Jack. She's demanding to see Max. I couldn't stop her from coming here."

There was an apologetic cough. "I'm sorry, Tony, but I'm under strict instructions not to let any journalists in, and in particular Alexis Banks."

Tony fixed Alexis with an "I told you so" glare, to which she snorted, "You didn't try hard enough. In fact, you didn't try at all." She leaned over his arm and projected her voice so she could be heard.

"Please ask Max to reconsider. It's an emergency. He must see me. Tell him if he doesn't, he'll be sorry."

"Uh . . ." There was a short pause and some background static as Jack seemed undecided.

"When this emergency blows up in Max's face, do

you honestly want to be the guy who let it happen?" Alexis demanded.

"Okay," Jack replied. "Can you just give me a minute? I'll go relay your message to the boss."

Max was in his mother's theater room, sipping cognac and watching television.

"I thought you were going back to Paris." His mother's voice floated over to him from her armchair across the room.

"I've put it off."

"Why?"

"Why not?"

His eyes left the screen so that he could look at her. "I thought you enjoyed having me here."

"I do." She paused, looking up from her book. "When you're not as grouchy as a bear."

He returned his attention to the television. Not that he was really watching. The noise washed over his cluttered brain as he brooded about the other problems in his life. The ones his mother didn't understand. She thought she did. But she didn't.

Suddenly, an advertisement for the latest issue of *Woman's Day* magazine came onto the screen, and Max saw himself locked in a passionate embrace with the woman he had been running from all week. He couldn't believe speculation was still rife three days later.

Abruptly he reached for the remote control and snapped the television off. But it was too late. The image had already burned itself onto his retinas.

Alexis's body arched in surrender.

Her long, dark hair rippling in the wind.

Her fingers entwined in the hair at the nape of his neck as her dark lashes fluttered closed.

There was no escape from Alexis Banks. Bad enough that she haunted his dreams. Now she consumed his waking moments as well. It was his mother's voice that broke his brooding silence. He looked up in annoyance to find that she had been studying his actions curiously.

"It just seems awfully peculiar to me," she began slowly, "that you won't talk to her, yet you linger here in Sydney keeping tabs on her. If you want nothing to do with the girl, why bother staying?"

Why, indeed?

Guilt, curiosity, sadistic need. A self-mocking smile curled his mouth. It was that kiss. He couldn't get it out of his head—or the haunted look on her face when she said, *Revenge will not make you feel any better, Max.*

She had been right about that. But, hell, he wasn't going to let himself be vulnerable to her. If he saw her again, she would sap his will just as she had on the porch and very nearly on the phone a few days ago. He couldn't trust her. Hell, he couldn't trust himself. He would keep his bodyguards on her for the sake of the kids. But communication—that was out of the question.

There was knock on the door, and Max glanced across the room as his mother's head of security walked in.

"Sir?"

"Yes."

"Er . . . Alexis Banks is here, and she is demanding to see you."

Involuntarily, his heart jumped in his chest. "Here?"

"At the front gate, sir."

His mouth dried at the very thought of her so close. Excitement and pain rippled through him simultaneously.

"She says it's an emergency."

His right hand tore into his hair and clenched a fistful. The urge to see her was strong. Very strong. And for that very reason, he couldn't. Seeing her again would only cause the feelings he was trying to suppress to surge up again. Who was he kidding? They were already up, fogging his brain with wanting.

He swore roughly at his own weakness. The guard, who thought it was directed at him, took a step back.

"I'm sorry, sir. She said you'd regret it if I didn't tell you."

Max dropped his hand from his head. "Send her away," he returned abruptly.

"Yes, sir." The guard took another step back. "At once, sir."

Just as the guard turned away, his mother looked up from her magazine. "No, Jack, wait."

The guard stopped and slowly turned around. "Ma'am?"

"Max may not wish to see Alexis. But *I* do."

Max's gaze snapped sharply to his mother. "You can't be serious."

"What?" Ceilia's gaze dropped innocently back to the

magazine she had been reading. "I have a right to meet the woman who has gotten my son so worked up."

Max's anger, which he thought he had cooled to a mild twenty degrees suddenly jumped to a hundred. "You don't understand what you're doing."

But his mother was choosing this of all moments not to be fobbed off. "On the contrary," she replied with cool certainty, "I think I do." There was nothing weak about the steel blue gaze that met his. "This is *my* house, Max and *I* shall invite in whomever I please. If you do not wish to see her, then leave the room. I have no intention of stopping you."

A cutting silence followed that remark. If she had been any other person, he would have strangled her.

Leave the room? Not on your life!

Who knew what manipulative ploy Alexis would deal out if he left her alone with his mother? Taking his long silence for acquiesce, Ceilia nodded to the guard. "Show her in, Jack."

When Alexis was ushered into the Ceilia's theater room by a scared-looking security guard, the first thing she saw was Max by the window with his back to her.

He's here.

At the gate, the guard had said that it was Ceilia Deroux who wanted to see her. She had not hoped to lay eyes on Max. For moment, all she could do was stare hungrily at his broad shoulders encased in white linen. His hands were buried deep in the pockets of his blue jeans, emphasizing his lean hips. He gave no indication that he had heard her come in, confining his gaze to whatever was in the garden.

"Alexis?"

A woman's voice broke her trance, and Alexis immediately turned to greet a blond woman who could only be Max's mother. They had the same intense blue eyes. She was seated on the sofa to the left and had not risen.

Alexis cleared her throat, shifting her bag more securely onto her shoulder. "Yes, that's me." She walked over to the sofa and held out her hand. "Nice to meet you, Mrs. Deroux."

Ceilia did not take her hand. "I wish I could say the same thing about you, my dear."

The dart hit home, and Alexis immediately dropped her hand. This wasn't going to be an easy interview. She should have seen it coming. In her book, a man enraged was much easier to deal with than a mature woman harboring cool anger.

Ceilia eyed her from head to foot with a kind of curious disdain. "You have caused nothing but trouble in my son's life since you entered it."

Alexis's eyes narrowed. "Is that why you wanted to see me?" she asked. "To berate me for what you think I've done?"

"Don't you think you deserve it?"

Alexis felt a blush infuse her face. "As I have tried to explain to Max, I was tricked just as much as he was. A colleague of mine wrote the magazine article without my knowledge."

"But you did the interview," Ceilia accused.

"Mrs. Deroux, I have two children. Two children I would do anything for. Their welfare is my life. You've had children of your own. Surely you would know how I feel."

Ceilia paused. "I was unaware that you had children."

"Technically, they are my sister's children. She died, and now they are mine. I needed the money for them. When I did that interview with Max, I had nothing in my head but that."

"And after the interview . . ."

"I couldn't write the article," Alexis said adamantly. "Not after I met Max, spoke to him . . ."—her eyes flew involuntarily to the window—". . . connected with him."

Still Max gave no indication that he had even registered her presence. Anger began to simmer under the surface of her determined front.

"I don't understand how your colleague got the information for the article without your knowledge."

Alexis winced guiltily. "I recorded the interview on tape. My ex-friend, Sandra, who works at *Starbuzz Magazine,* was babysitting that night. After I got home, I told her I didn't want to do the article anymore, and I broke the tape in half and dropped it in a wastebasket. While I was checking on the twins, she showed herself out. But before she left, she must have picked up the tape and taken it with her."

"You broke it in half?"

"Yes."

"I guess if the actual tape wasn't cut, it would be

easy enough to glue the plastic casing back together and salvage the material."

"Unfortunately, yes."

"So you really didn't write that article?"

"No."

"And you really had no intention of doing so?"

"No."

"And you didn't get a cent for it?"

Alexis looked down at her old jeans and worn sneakers. "Does it look like I got a cent for it?"

"I guess not."

"She's lying!" Both women's heads turned to the enraged voice at the window. Finally Max had turned around. His gaze ripped through Alexis like an electric shock.

"You can't trust her."

"You want to believe that, Max," Alexis choked unsteadily. "Because you can't face being wrong about me."

"You're a journalist," he accused.

"Yes, I am." Alexis nodded. "But I'm not responsible for your sister's death."

His eyes raked her with disgust. "Stop pretending that you know me, because you don't."

"I know guilt when I see it. Don't forget that I've been there too."

He cast her a look that could have incinerated steel and then strode across the room to where she stood. The very air seemed to sizzle in his wake. She didn't know whether to be frightened or aroused.

"I don't want to see you. I don't want to talk to you. I want you out of my life."

His words were as sharp as arrows, but she lifted her chin bravely.

"I am happy to leave you alone. In fact, nothing would please me more than for my life to get back to the way it was. But I can't do that without your help."

"Why should I help you?"

"Because if you don't, I'll lose the children."

Her words seems to catch him off guard, and for a moment he said nothing.

"What are you talking about?"

"I could lose custody of the girls because of this."

He looked heavenward and then back at her. "Is this some warped attempt to try to extort more out of me? Because—"

"It's the truth, you idiot!" Alexis exclaimed. "And I have proof." She immediately opened her handbag and withdrew the letter from Paul's lawyer, shoving it into his hands.

Reluctantly, he lifted the paper and scanned it.

"I can't get a job, I can barely pay the rent, and my every move is being watched by the media, who believe I am your mistress," she informed him. "You could say that you've handed the children to my brother-in-law on a silver platter. Now it's your job to undo the damage."

Max handed the letter to his mother—who was trying, somewhat unsubtly, to read it over his shoulder—and fixed Alexis with an obnoxious glare. It was hard to believe that he was the same man who had wined and dined her at Crusades.

"Is your brother-in-law a decent man?"

Alexis blinked at this unexpected question. "I— What do you mean?"

"Can he or can he not take care of children?"

"I suppose he can, but—"

"Is he financially and emotionally able to take care of children?"

"Yes, but—"

"Then what's the problem?" he taunted her. "They're probably better off with him anyway. If I were you, I would count my lucky stars they had somewhere decent to go."

Alexis felt as if she had been slapped in the face. Tears smarted at the back of her eyes, but she blinked hastily before they flowed forward. There was no way that she was crying in front of him. No way. Hell would freeze over before she showed him any kind of weakness.

"My sister and her husband chose me." She clenched her fists by her sides to stop herself from shaking. "That was what they wanted. Do you know why?"

"Enlighten me." The request was clearly contemptuous.

"Because they knew I would do my best to keep their memory alive. Paul and Lisa can't have children of their own. Paul doesn't want to help his brother; he wants to replace him. And why would Lisa tell the twins about their mother when she never liked Mel in the first place?"

"That's ridiculous."

Alexis's mouth hardened. "They were always jealous of my sister and her husband from day one. They coveted what they couldn't have. Now they intend to have it all and cut me out of the twins' lives as well. I can't let that happen."

"Maybe you don't have a choice."

She lifted her chin with determination. "People always have choices, and if you think I'm going to let those kids forget their mother, especially when—" She broke off.

"When what?"

She hesitated. "When I'm the one responsible for her death."

His brief laugh was cruel. "I thought you didn't blame yourself."

"I lied."

"So you think you need to make some sort of atonement?"

"Takes one to know one," she shot back. "I would have thought you of all people would understand."

"Well, you're out of luck, Alexis, because I'm with the lawyers. Give them to the guy who deserves them."

"Okay, that's enough!" They both spun around to see that Ceilia Deroux had been watching their exchange with growing disgust. "I've heard enough to know that you have both behaved very badly in this situation. You need to put your differences aside and . . ."

"Mother." Max rolled a furious glance in her direction. "What are you doing?"

"I—"

"This *situation*, as you so refer to it, has absolutely nothing to do with you, and I think you have interfered enough."

"Max, this is not right. You know it's not right," Ceilia protested. "You're not acting yourself."

"You don't understand," he accused her. "You have never understood. I shouldn't have stayed here to humor you. That was my first mistake. I will leave you to your . . ." He cast Alexis a contemptuous look before he ground out his final word. ". . . *guest.*"

He strode from the room, taking all hope with him.

Paralyzed by this anticlimax, Alexis was left standing there staring at the floor in utter desolation.

Ceilia held out her letter to her. "I'm sorry, my dear."

Alexis took the letter, folded it, and then slowly looked up. "If he thinks this is over, he's wrong. I'll do whatever it takes to keep those children, with or without his consent. He'll be sorry for this. Very sorry."

"My dear—" Ceilia began.

But Alexis stuffed the letter back into her handbag, turned on her heel, and left the room as well.

Alexis brooded all the way home. She had to face facts. Max wasn't going to help her just because she asked him to. He wasn't even going to talk to her just because she wanted him to.

I don't want to see you. I don't want to talk to you. I want you out of my life.

Well, if he didn't want to help her, she was just going to have to make him. She wasn't giving up custody of the twins. She still had two weeks to bring Max around to her way of thinking. The only way to topple the idiot off his high horse was to fight fire with fire. In fact, she didn't know why she hadn't thought of it before.

After Tony brought her home and she paid off the babysitter, she marched straight to her bedroom. Kneeling down on the floor, she lifted the dust ruffle on her bed and pulled out a small chest that was underneath it. It was full of sentimental items that had belonged to her sister and her sister's husband. The majority of their assets had been sold to pay the debts her sister's husband had left behind. But there were still a few small trinkets left for the twins, so that they would have something of their parents when they were older. Lifting the lid, she pulled out a small jewelry box that was sitting on top of a pile of photo albums and opened it.

A beautiful white-gold ring sat in a bed of satin. She held it up to the light. It was truly a work of art, intricate in design and classical in beauty. A circuit of small diamonds circled a sapphire the size of her knuckle. It had been her sister's engagement ring, but before that it had been her sister's mother-in-law's engagement ring. It was an heirloom—an heirloom that belonged to the twins. An heirloom that she would never sell to help them get by. Maybe things were tight right now, but the twins would not be deprived of this small inheritance. It was more than just a ring. It was all they had left of their parents, and she would not take it from them. Of course, she wasn't averse to borrowing it . . . just for a little while.

She slid the ring on and lifted her hand to admire the effect. What did Paul's lawyer say she lacked? Financial and emotional security. Hah! She'd see about that, and so would Max. Before the week was out, he would be pulling out all the stops just to talk to her.

Or to stop her talking.

Max had never been so angry in his life. He was angry at Alexis, he was angry at his mother, and he was angry at himself. The degree of his anger toward each of the three persons varied as he recalled different aspects of his conversation with Alexis the day before. How had life gotten so complicated? Last month, revenge looked sweet, his mother was demure, and he had absolutely no doubt about how he felt. Now revenge tasted bitter, his mother was too opinionated, and every time Alexis walked into a room, he had the irrational urge to grab her by the shoulders and kiss her senseless. His latent feelings for her were driving him mad. He had to keep reminding himself how he *should* be reacting to her. Wanting to kiss her *shouldn't* be a response to her presence, although on the plus side, at least it would shut her up.

His mother hadn't help things when she apologized to him that morning and promised never to get involved again. That only served to make him feel like a jerk for yelling at her when she had just been worried and sad.

"Are you sure you're okay?" she had asked.

He had too much pride to say, "No, I'm not okay. I've

never been so confused in my life," and so had adopted the silence of a martyr.

He didn't know whether he'd done the right thing. Had he been too hard on Alexis? After sleeping on her words—or should he say, *not* sleeping on her words— some of what she said started to seem plausible. She could have been doubled-crossed just as she had explained. His mother had certainly believed her. Dare he trust her for the sake of the children?

The children.

He couldn't deny their existence. He'd seen them with his own eyes. Cute little things. Innocent, unknowing. Now pawns in a chess game. Clearly, if he didn't help Alexis, they would be handed over to their uncle. Even if Paul Grant was a good man, any kind of uprooting like that was always hard on kids, and they'd already been through it once when their parents died.

But what did she expect from him? The truth was, he had already tried to tell the media that they weren't lovers. They didn't believe him. In fact, the more he denied it, the more they thought he was hiding something. They refused to be put off by words alone. As for the whole job thing, he hadn't made any attempt to block her getting assignments as a journalist, despite his original plan to make sure she never worked again. If *Starbuzz Magazine* had fired her, it wasn't because of him. He couldn't understand why she couldn't get work. Any other magazine would snap her up in a second just to get the rest of the story.

The inspiration he'd had for a song the day before had

deserted him, and for the remainder of the afternoon he sat listlessly in the theater room, tapping a pencil against a blank pad. His mother joined him at about three with tea and scones. But he wasn't interested in food.

"You know," Ceilia began tentatively, "She told me before she left that she's going to fight you on this."

He immediately looked up from his pad, not even needing to ask who "She" was before jumping into his first question. "What do you mean, fight me on this? There's nothing to fight about. She can't force me to help her."

"She thinks she can."

Suddenly there was a rap at the door, and the ever-suffering security guard walked in with a grim look on his face. "Er . . . Mrs. Deroux, apparently, there is a news bulletin on Channel Three that might interest you and your son."

Ceilia picked up the remote control on the coffee table and switched on their large flat-screen television.

The security guard was right. Max watched the television, mesmerized as the scene unfolded.

An excited female reporter was running down a Sydney street to catch up with a slender, sexy woman, whom he immediately recognized as Alexis Banks.

"Ms. Banks, Ms. Banks! Is it true? Can you confirm the rumors?"

Alexis Banks spun around as the reporter put a microphone under her mouth, her left hand pressed to her cheek in surprise that was clearly artificial.

"What rumors?"

Max growled.

What is she doing?

Doesn't she realize that talking to them just encourages them?

Where is her bodyguard?

Then he saw what she so strategically was trying to show the camera and anyone who happened to be watching. He gasped as the reporter continued to question her.

"Is it true that you are engaged to Max Deroux?"

Alexis's smile was coy as she flicked her glossy hair over one shoulder. "We haven't made a formal announcement yet . . . but, yes . . . yes, we're engaged."

"What!!!!!"

Max saw red. Yet he couldn't tear his gaze from the screen as the scene changed back to the news desk.

"There you have it," a wide-eyed blond woman reported. "Confirmation from Alexis Banks that she is indeed engaged to Max Deroux. The community has been rife with speculation ever since she was first seen sporting the gorgeous sapphire engagement ring yesterday afternoon. Witnesses say that preparation for the wedding is already under way. This morning Alexis Banks was also seen at an exclusive bridal shop in central Sydney with her bodyguard and later at a café, flicking through wedding magazines. It seems this supercouple is wasting no time. We are yet to receive comment from Max Deroux."

No surprise there.

He had reporters turned away as a matter of course.

Who knew that this time he'd actually want to know what questions they were asking? He had to breathe deeply to stop his blood from boiling.

"What in blazin' hell does she want from me?" he demanded more of himself then anyone else, but his mother decided to answer.

"Your attention, clearly."

His gaze snapped to her smug expression. "Go on, say it." He waved at her. "I know you're dying to. You might as well get it off your chest."

"Well . . ." Ceilia shrugged. "She did ask nicely, and you refused to listen. You can't blame the girl for trying harder. You know, all you had to do was set a few rumors straight. Why couldn't you do that? What are you so afraid of?"

"Mother, I don't think you quite get it. This woman broke into your home, cornered me in a room under false pretenses, taped our conversation, and then wrote an article about it. She's dangerous."

"But you like her."

"No, I—" He spun on his heel as words failed him.

Ceilia stood up as he headed for the door. "Darling, where are you going?"

"To break up with my fiancée!"

Chapter Seven

By the time Max reached Alexis's run-down house in Hornsby, his rage was so complete that, had someone touched him, they would have received an electric shock. He was furious about the engagement story. Furious because it had bought him to her doorstep, just as she wanted. And furious because she was still living in that decrepit old house when the least she could do was the spend the gold she had taken such pains to dig and move out.

It was Tony who greeted him somewhat nervously at the door.

"Good evening, Mr. Deroux."

A camera flashed from the bushes.

Max nodded in acknowledgment and then rapped loudly on the door. "Alexis!"

A minute later the door swung open, and a very unimpressed Alexis stood on the threshold, her hands on her hips and her head cocked to one side. Dressed casually in shorts and a T-shirt, she still managed to entice him like an exotic fruit, and his senses took the full blast of seeing her again. Her legs and feet were bare, and the silky tresses of her hair were caught up in a loose bun that exposed the slender line of her neck. He felt his focus shift involuntarily to the soft curve between her ear and shoulder, which just begged for a man's lips. His lips.

He scowled.

Damn the woman.

Kissing Alexis's bloody neck should be the last thing on his mind. Abruptly he walked past her into the house, ignoring her gasp of protest.

Two little girls were on the floor to his right, playing with their Barbies. They stopped playing and looked up at him with distrust.

"What do you think you're doing?" Alexis's voice was shrill. "This is my house, and you can't just walk in here like you own the place."

He spun around, his voice dark with purpose. "Well, as your husband-to-be, this place is almost half-mine, isn't it?"

He saw her eyes flicker worriedly toward the children.

"I have no idea what you're talking about."

"So we're playing that game, are we?"

His peripheral vision caught shadows moving below, and he looked down. Two small heads, bent back as far as their necks could take, looked up at him from a position somewhere near his knees. They seemed to be studying him carefully, trying to make an assessment of his character.

Was he a good person?

Should he be talking to their aunt?

Even in their innocence he could see the thoughts flickering across their faces, making his gut flip uneasily. Suddenly one of them clasped her hands together in front of her belly. "Do you like hamsters?" she asked.

The question, while not even vaguely related to any of the thoughts spinning in his head, was serious. He knew beyond the shadow of a doubt that it was a test. The wrong answer would damn him forever. The correct answer would lift their opinion of him to the highest of levels.

He replied without hesitation. "Yes."

Huge smiles spread across their little faces, and the one who had asked him the question said, "Auntie Alex is going to take Kayla and me to Hamsterdam to buy one."

He blinked. "Hamsterdam?"

"Only if we're good." Kayla tried to ease his confusion. "And we eat our beans."

"I see." Max couldn't help but warm to their innocence. "Beans are very hard to eat."

"Not as hard as carrots." The first sister shook her head vigorously, and he had to suppress a smile. It was at this point that Alexis joined them.

"Holly, Kayla." She touched their heads. "It's almost dinnertime. Will you please go wash your hands?"

As the twins reluctantly left the room, she turned

back to him and said, "I wish you'd come when they were sleeping. This is not a conversation we can have in front of them."

"Depends on what the conversation is, really." Max shrugged. "I'm here to say two things. Take that ring off your finger, and stop spreading rumors."

Alexis raised an eyebrow. "Or you'll do what? Kiss me again in front of the cameras? Somehow I don't think it'll work so well the second time around."

He gritted his teeth. He should just kiss her right now. That would teach her!

Teach her what?

That he found her irresistible? He groaned inwardly. That would be playing right into her hands. The temptation, no matter how palpable, had to be resisted.

"Well?" She raised her eyebrows.

"This is not a game, Alexis. You need to stop being so difficult. I thought we had an understanding. You stay out of my life, and I'll stay out of yours."

"I don't recall any such understanding." Her expressive brown eyes flashed. "What I do recall is you being unreasonable and my being forced to . . . take extreme measures."

"Has anyone ever told you how absolutely infuriating you are?"

"No," she replied infuriatingly. "Never."

He groaned.

"Ready!" The twins tore back into the room and circled their legs. Kayla tugged on Max's pants legs. "Are you staying for dinner?"

"No," Max said at the same time that Alexis said, "Yes."

"Don't be silly, Max," she added sweetly. "We need time to talk about this properly—perhaps later, when the twins are playing. You need to stay. Don't you want to plan our future?"

She lay her left hand provocatively against the base of her throat so that the engagement ring was clearly visible for his inspection. He felt a muscle in his cheek twitch as he clenched his teeth.

Clearly, she was pulling out all the stops to be heard. But the last time he'd "talked" to this woman, he'd confessed his deepest secrets, and she'd published them in a gossip magazine. Did she honestly think he was going to be sucked into that again? Better to leave now and come back later when his anger had cooled and the children were in bed.

But Kayla grabbed one hand, and Holly grabbed the other, and they pulled him to the table. Short of flinging them both off, he could do nothing but comply.

Women! They were sly creatures, no matter what the age.

Alexis could not believe that Max Deroux was sitting at her kitchen table. If someone had told her a month ago that this would happen, she would have laughed in their face. Dressed in designer jeans and a black collared shirt, he was every inch the megastar of a female's fantasies. But there he was, sitting at her old pine table, his forearms resting lightly by his floral print plate that matched no other plate on the table. She was still living like a student, preferring to spend money on more important things than a dinner set.

The twins had obviously fallen for him, because they chattered to him excitedly, each one fighting for his attention. Despite not having any children of his own, he seemed to handle them with gentle ease—a circumstance that both annoyed and impressed her.

Is everyone better at this than me?

Every now and then he glanced at her, looking for an opening to get the topic back to why he was really there. She made sure he didn't get one. She wanted to give him a chance to calm down. A rational Max would be easier to appease than an incensed one. Besides, after dinner the kids would move back to their toys, and she would be able to speak to him without two pairs of inquisitive ears listening in.

Alexis moved to fetch her shepherd's pie out of the oven and sighed when she saw it. The meat was burned and the mash was watery. Cooking had been Mel's department—the domestic queen, the perfect mother. All Alexis knew how to make was cocktails, thanks to her extensive bar experience in Europe. It was so hard to follow in Mel's impeccable footsteps. As a single woman without responsibilities, she had survived on salads and toast in between the occasional takeout. But she couldn't do that with the kids. They needed a wholesome diet, not meals on the go. So she had been picking up free recipe cards at the supermarket—not that they'd helped her much, as Max would soon find out.

She took the pie and set it in the center of the table. Kayla and Holly pulled faces.

"Don't be rude, girls."

But she made sure not to look at Max as she cut through the burnt cheese on the top with a knife.

"Plates." She held out her hand. The twins passed her theirs one by one. She filled each plate with the required amount, trying to ignore the way it slopped out of shape as soon as it left her spatula. Finally she filled Max's plate and her own.

"Smells good."

At his words, Alexis looked up and finally met his eyes. They were dancing wickedly. He was enjoying her discomfort with a boy's mischief. Her heart fluttered unexpectedly, and she hurriedly looked away as she sat down. In her haste, her legs accidentally collided with his, which were stretched out under the table.

"Sorry," they both said at exactly the same time and drew in their legs.

The twins giggled.

"Eat your dinner, girls."

Alexis watched as Kayla and Holly picked up their forks and stuck them into their food. But neither of them tasted her pie. Max picked up his fork, speared a mouthful, and popped it into his mouth. He choked, spluttered, and then swallowed with difficulty.

Alexis sat forward. "Are you okay?"

"Fine, fine." However, she noticed that he wouldn't meet her eyes.

Carefully she tasted her own meal.

Nuts. I knew I put in too much salt.

"Now I know why you wanted me to stay for dinner."

She couldn't help it; a smile turned up the corners of her mouth. "As mad as I've been with you this past week, I didn't do this on purpose." She grimaced as she looked down. "I don't think *anyone* could do this on purpose."

"May we go?" Holly asked.

"But you haven't touched your meal."

"I don't like it," said Kayla.

Alexis felt tears smarting behind her eyes and hastily blinked. It had been a bad week all around. But this was not the time to let it all get to her.

"Why don't we order pizza?" Max suggested.

"Yay!" The girls jumped up and down in their seats.

If only it were that simple.

"We can't afford pizza," she replied tightly.

"What about the money you got for the article?"

Her fork clattered to her plate.

Back to square one.

"Here we go again." She stood up, removing the pie from the table and taking it to the sink. She heard his chair scrape back and his footsteps behind her.

"Why haven't you moved out of this place?"

She ignored him and began clearing away dishes and wiping down the counter. What was the point, anyway? She might as well spare her breath. Warm hands clasped her shoulders and spun her to face him.

"Leave that. I'm talking to you."

She looked up into turbulent blue eyes. A flush heated her skin. He just didn't get it, did he?

"Why haven't you used the money?"

She searched his face for a hint of understanding and found none.

"Alexis, answer me."

"Max," she replied with painstaking slowness, "tell me what it is I have to say to you to make you believe I didn't write that article, because I'm at my wit's end. I honestly don't know how I can get through to you anymore."

His silence was telling, and she swallowed the lump in her throat. "Is it really so impossible for you to believe me? Do you hate me that much?"

"Alex." It was the first time he shortened her name, and it whispered off his lips like a sigh. His hands dropped from her shoulders. "I don't . . ." He looked away from her for a second, trying to find words. Then his gaze returned to hers, and she had to suck in a breath at what she saw there. "I don't . . ." He reached up and laid a palm on her cheek. "I don't hate you."

Time seemed to stand still as they gazed into each other's eyes, searching for meaning and perhaps something more.

"Are you going to kiss her now?"

The whispered words made them both freeze and look down. Kayla and Holly were standing in between them, looking up with undisguised excitement on their faces.

"Uh . . ." Max's hand left her cheek and did a small arc over his head to scratch the back of his neck. "How about we get that pizza now?"

"But—"

"No buts," he silenced Alexis's protests. "My treat."

After a small debate over toppings, they rang a local outlet and organized for two pizzas and a large garlic bread to be delivered to the house. As soon as that was settled, the twins went back to the living room and their Barbies to wait. It would be a good thirty minutes before dinner arrived.

Alexis and Max were left staring at each other in the kitchen.

"Would you like tea or coffee?" she asked, eager to reduce the tension in the room.

"No, I'm fine." He sat down at the table again, playing with the corner of a placemat. She came to join him, and he met her gaze as she also sat down.

"So, what are we going to do?" he asked.

"I don't know. I guess that's up to you." She paused, silently begging him to see things her way. "What's it going to be, Max? Are you going to help me, or are we going to be at each other's throats forever?"

It was in that moment that he realized that he didn't want that at all. It was too exhausting, not to mention dangerous. Every time he saw her, he felt his feelings grow. It was becoming next to impossible to stop them.

Alexis was about as close to her breaking point as cracked glass. You couldn't fake that kind of desperation. He'd seen the tears she blinked back when she'd removed the pie from the oven, heard the pleading in her voice when she'd spoken to the children, felt her despair when she'd said to him, *Tell me what it is I have to say to you to make you believe . . .*

He still had his reservations about her. But he'd seen too much and felt too much that evening not to be affected.

He glanced over at the children playing together in the living room, completely oblivious to the fact that their fate was in his hands. He knew what his responsibilities were. He couldn't walk away even if he wanted to.

"I want to do the right thing by the children," he said slowly. "I don't want them to fall into their uncle's care if it's going to be a bad thing for them."

She let out a small sigh of relief. "So you'll help me?"

"Yes." He smirked at his own words, mocking himself rather than her. "Yes, I'll help you."

"I don't mean to tempt fate," she said slowly. "But may I ask why?"

His eyes ran over her worried countenance. Now, of all times, she didn't trust him. How ironic, especially when he'd just decided to believe her.

"Seeing you living like this . . ." He hesitated, not wanting to reveal how easily she could tug at his heartstrings. "Well . . . the story you told my mother just seemed to come together. I believe you. I believe you didn't write that article."

Her breath whooshed out as though she'd been holding it. "That means a lot to me."

He shrugged, not really knowing what to say. *You've won this battle, but you won't win the war?*

She traced a finger around the pattern on her old tablecloth as she contemplated her next move. He found the unconscious action very sensual and shifted uncomfortably in his seat. The fire he had managed to put out just in time suddenly burst alight again.

Stop it.

"We need a plan," she said.

He sat up straight at her words, hoping to goodness that his face didn't show anything of what he'd been thinking.

"Yes."

She twisted the engagement ring off her finger and set it between them. "This was just a ploy to get your attention. I'll set the media straight, if you tell them that the kiss was a setup and to back off. If I can just get the cameras out of my life, I might be able to fix my job situation. Do you think you can do that?"

This was going to be harder than he'd thought. "I'm afraid that's not possible."

Her eyes widened. "What do you mean? I thought you were going to help me."

"I am. But we're already too far gone for that."

"How far gone?"

He pushed a frustrated hand into his hair. "The truth is, I've already tried talking to the media. I tried to get them to back off days ago. The media don't believe me any more than they believe you. The fact is, they're not going to back off until they get their story."

Her fingers curled into her palm, and he felt her panic as clearly as if it were his own.

"Then Paul will get the children. It's all over."

He frowned grimly. He should have known it would come to this. Maybe subconsciously he had been aware of it all along. She had backed him sweetly into a corner. And for the sake of the children, he had to go along with it.

He picked up the ring and her hand and slid the cool metal band back onto her finger, ignoring the awareness that tingled up his arm at the first touch. As soon as the deed was done, he removed his hands.

"This is all we've got, and you know it."

She blinked. "You can't be serious."

"This is what you've wanted all along, isn't it?"

"I beg your pardon."

"Why go for a measly fifty grand when you could have it all?"

Her chair scraped back as she stood up in haste. "Are you implying what I think you're implying?"

"Just because I believe you didn't write that article doesn't mean I trust you."

She laughed hysterically. "Oh, believe me, that's apparent!"

"Alexis, sit down."

But she ignored the order.

"So now you think I'm after your money?"

"I don't know. You tell me."

She threw up her hands. "Great! Just great. So, what? I'm supposed to be manipulating you into marriage so I can get my grimy little hands on all your worldly goods?"

His lips turned up at the corners. He didn't seriously believe it. But he couldn't help testing her a little. She was, after all, a journalist.

"It's not a bad plan . . . if your victim's an idiot."

"Well, then, I probably would have gotten pretty far with you, wouldn't I?" she retorted scornfully.

His lips twitched. "Wow, you do pack a good punch, don't you?"

She continued as though he hadn't spoken. "I wouldn't propose to you if you were the last man on earth."

"My goodness," he remarked cynically. "And here I was, thinking you were capable of just about anything."

She glared at him. "Trust you to rub it in my face. I admit, I have acted a little shamelessly lately, but—"

"A *little*?"

"But I would never seriously ask this of you." She began to tug at the ring on her finger, but he put a hand on her wrist to stop her.

"And neither would I," he said grimly. "But a pretend engagement is not out of the question."

She stopped tugging on the ring. "Really?" She raised an eyebrow. "You would do that?"

He shrugged. "A pretend engagement is the smartest and easiest way to get the lawyers off your back. If you marry me, you'll have emotional and financial security, which will make the fact that you don't have a job redundant. I can easily convince your brother-in-law that his arguments no longer stand. In any event, the media will certainly cover it."

"And you'd go along with that?"

"For the children, yes." He frowned. "The problem is making it look convincing."

She shook her head. "They already believe me. The media is all over this."

"Yeah, but the courts and your brother-in-law aren't. They'll dig a little deeper." He took a deep breath, trying to center himself but instead achieving a pair of lungs full of vanilla and coconut—Alexis's signature scent. It only seemed to make matters worse when his next words came out somewhat huskily.

"You'll have to move in with me."

"Move in with you?" Alexis squeaked.

And immediately she had a flash of Max in a pair of black satin pajamas. Not that she knew what color his pajamas were or whether they were indeed satin. He might not wear any at all, for goodness' sake. She swallowed with difficulty.

Get a grip! You're way off the mark.

He seemed to recognize her sudden increase in tension, because he added quickly, "My mother's house has heaps of rooms. You won't lack for privacy—believe me."

She blushed. Of course she wouldn't. She was being completely irrational. After all, this was a business arrangement. That house was huge, and there would be maids and other house staff roaming around in the corridors as well, not to mention his mother! Moving in with him would be like moving into an apartment house. There was no need to get all hot under the collar. Yet she still rubbed the back of her neck uncomfortably.

"What about the children?"

"They'll come too, of course."

"And your mother? She won't like this."

"Believe me, if I hadn't offered first, my mother would be next in line. She's been giving me disapproving looks since you spoke to her."

"Are you sure?"

"Positive. We need this to look convincing."

Living with Max Deroux in his mother's mansion. As she repeated the words to herself, they seemed surreal. If she couldn't buy it, who else was going to?

"I can't do it."

He frowned. "What?"

"I just can't."

It's way too close for comfort.

"Well, you can't stay here."

It was her turn to glare at him. "Why not?"

"Alexis," Max began with awful patience, "we are trying to prove that you are financially secure."

"I'm sure we can still do that without—"

"Alexis." He leaned forward. "If I loved you, loved you enough to marry you, do you honestly think I'd let you live here?"

She swallowed as the word *love* slipped over her heart, cruel and kind at the same time. She sighed inwardly. To be loved by him . . . It was a dream, no more.

You would be lucky to be liked *by him.*

She looked away, using the time to restart her voice box. "What's wrong with this place?"

"What isn't?"

He scanned the room as though searching for something to compliment but not finding anything.

"O-kay." Her voice came out strained as she realized

she was running out of excuses—logical ones, anyway. "I get it. I'll . . . The girls and I will move into your mother's mansion."

"Make that tonight."

"But—"

"Pack an overnight bag. We can get the rest of your stuff tomorrow."

She felt as if she were on a roller coaster and couldn't get off.

He stood up, seeming to enjoy the control as he ticked items off on his fingers. "We'll probably need to be seen in public a few times. Maybe I should make a formal media statement. You can call your brother-in-law and tell him to back off. If you're not up to it, I could always step in. And . . ." He turned, his eyes focusing on her hand. "Where did you get that ring?"

Still back at his first point—*We'll probably need to be seen in public a few times*—she answered truthfully without thought. "It was my sister's."

"Then I'll have to get you a new one."

That caught her attention.

"Whatever for?" She clasped her hand to her chest. "This one's fine. I neither expect nor want you to do that."

"Your brother-in-law will recognize that ring. He'll see it as proof that this is a scam. We need to get one for us."

She winced. He was right, of course. Paul would recognize it. But she couldn't stand being so beholden to Max, especially when he thought so little of her. She pressed her lips together, trying to salvage what was left of her choices.

"It will be on loan only. I'm giving it back the second this is over."

He glanced at her impassively. "Of course."

"Hang on a minute." She suddenly saw the vital flaw in their plan. "When will it be over? We can't pretend to be engaged forever."

"No," he agreed. "So let's discuss the exit strategy."

Exit strategy? This was definitely a business arrangement.

He sat down again. "You will continue to look for a job, and as soon as you get one and have worked in it for the probationary period, thus proving financial security, we shall break off our engagement. You won't need it anymore."

"Right," she said slowly. "I get a steady job, and we get unengaged."

"Yes."

She nodded. "Sounds good."

"I just have one condition. You can't work as a journalist."

She gasped. It was a ruthless condition. "You can't do that."

He shrugged. "I just did."

It was then that she realized that, despite his offering of help, he still hadn't let his vendetta go. He still meant to punish her in a way that didn't affect the children. All this niceness was for them, not her.

"But I'm trained as a journalist!" she cried. "My degree is in journalism. How am I supposed to get a decent job if I can't apply for what I have training in?"

"I'm sure you'll think of something." His face was expressionless.

"Max, be reasonable."

"I am. Why on earth would I ask a journalist to marry me? I hate journalists. If you want to make this lie plausible, you have to let this go."

Great.

"There are plenty of good jobs out there that don't require degrees," he continued.

"You mean, like waitressing or office temping."

"Why not?"

"I've already tried to get jobs like that."

He raised his eyebrows in disbelief. "Well, clearly you didn't try hard enough."

He sounded exactly like Paul, and in that moment she hated him. How could he possibly understand what it was like? Mr. Designer-Label Mansion Man. He didn't have a clue. The twins made it impossible for her to hold down a job like that. The last place she had worked at had kept her for a month before they fired her. The twins had contracted chicken pox, and she had taken too much leave. She needed a job that was flexible, that she could take home if necessary. Journalism was perfect for that, and it was what she was trained to do.

"You know, you simply have no idea what my life is like. You—"

He held up a hand for silence. "I'm not going to change my mind. Do we have deal or not?"

She met his unyielding blue eyes, inwardly fuming. What choice did she have? She had less than two weeks to fix this problem. Holding the media back was not an option. Getting a job quickly and passing the probationary period was not an option. The only thing left was the engagement. She had to agree to his terms and buy herself some time.

Yes, that's how she should think of it. The engagement was a stalling mechanism. She would still have to fix the problem herself; she would just have more time to do it. If she thought about it that way . . . it seemed okay.

A knock at the door broke into her thoughts, and the twins dropped their dolls.

"Pizza!" they squealed.

She chuckled as they ran up and raced around her legs, tugging at her hands.

"Yes, yes, I know. I heard them too."

She looked up at Max, who was watching her watching them, and she felt the smile drop off her face.

Here was the crux of it. The children needed her. And he was doing this for them. It was the best chance they had.

"Okay." She nodded. "You have a deal."

"Shall we shake on it?" He held out his hand, and she lifted hers, placing it palm to palm. His fingers closed around hers with warm possession. She felt the zing clear to her toes and couldn't help but believe that she had just agreed to more than she'd bargained for.

Chapter Eight

After dinner, Max rang his mother. From his end of the conversation, Alexis could tell that not only was there going to be no protest from Ceilia, but the superstar mum was absolutely determined to make her new guests as comfortable as possible. Unable to handle his mother's countless instructions, Max passed his phone to Alexis and went to help the children pack.

"Hello?"

"Now you let Max handle everything, okay?" Ceilia began. "I don't want you stressing out. We have plenty of room here. The twins will love it. I want you to feel at home, so . . ."

Whatever else was said was lost as Max brought a small box of toys into the living room with the twins hot on his heels.

"They've said they want to take these, but I'm not sure what to pack in the way of clothes."

"Mrs. Deroux, may I call you back?"

The rest of the evening passed in a blur. Max watched the children, while Alexis retired to the bedrooms to pack a small bag of clothes for each of them. As she pulled her old backpacks out from under her bed, she couldn't help but sit back on her heels for a second and take a breather.

Was this really happening?

Was she moving in with a megastar?

The situation was all just a little too unreal.

However, when they exited the house, and the usual cameras flashed, she knew that, whether it was real or not, in less than twenty-four hours all of Sydney would know about it.

The pictures would be different this time, though. She imagined the scene as if she were looking at it from across the street. She and Max each had a twin by the hand. The girls were giggling and talking excitedly as they skipped beside them. Max had his other hand in the small of her back, guiding her protectively down the porch steps . . . as though he really cared. One of the bodyguards was carrying their bags; the other was locking up the house. It was clear they wouldn't be coming back for a while. How many times had she seen images like this in magazines? Celebrity families moving out, moving up, and moving on.

The word *family* stuck in her throat like a fishbone.

That's what they would look like when the story came out. The magazines would describe Max's desire to live with his fiancée and her children as though they had spoken about it with him personally. The article would be about as close to the truth as Mars was to Earth. Instantly she felt a little stupid about all the stories she had read in the past and accepted without question.

How many of those photos hid a story totally different from what had been published? And how was it any of her business, anyway?

The twins loved the limousine. They jumped into it as if it was the biggest treat they'd had all year. It probably wasn't far off the mark.

She glanced at Max, who was sprawled casually on the seat beside her. He looked completely undisturbed by the sudden turn of events.

He cocked an eyebrow under her scrutiny. "Second thoughts?"

"No . . ." She looked at her hands. "It's just . . . this is all moving so fast."

"Not really," he drawled. "I hear that sixty kilometers per hour is the speed limit in this area."

She rolled her eyes but made no reply.

"Where are we going?" Holly piped up.

"My place," said Max.

"Why?"

He smiled. "Because it's fun."

Holly's eyes widened. "Do you live in Hamsterdam?"

"Uh . . . no," Max replied. "But I swear you'll love it just the same."

Holly grinned, and Alexis felt a sudden stab of guilt as Paul's words came back to her.

The twins have just lost their parents. They need a stable environment. You can't be introducing your passing flings to them left, right, and center. What if they got attached to one of them?

This wasn't a fling. But Paul was right about not letting the twins get attached to men who would only be in their life for a short time. It was not only irresponsible, it was cruel. And Max was definitely going to grace their lives for only a short time.

Ceilia was all smiles when they arrived, greeting them warmly in the hall.

"Just take those bags straight upstairs," she directed the bodyguards. "You must be tired." She patted Alexis's hand. She glanced down at the children, whose initial excitement had rapidly fizzled. They were both yawning.

"Thank you so much for letting us stay here." Alexis pressed her hand back. "I really don't know what to say. You really don't owe—"

"Let's not talk about that now, dear," Ceilia interrupted. "We need to get you up to your rooms."

A giant king bed adorned the center of Alexis's room with embroidered white linens and a dark wood headboard. It was flanked by matching bedside chests of drawers, one topped by a pretty reading lamp, the other with a vase of fragrant white lilies. To the right of the bed was a set of glass double doors leading out to a balcony that presented a magnificent view of the lake. Alexis took a deep, satisfying breath as she sat down on the bed.

Luxurious was an understatement.

She had her own bathroom, and there was a door that led directly into the bedroom next door, where the twins would be sleeping. A room almost as perfect as her own, with two single beds dressed in pale pink and quaint white wardrobes.

Max walked in through the connecting door. "Mum is settling the kids."

She stood up. "I should go to them."

"Wait. Just one minute." He lightly grabbed her shoulders as she would have walked past him.

She stopped and looked up.

His allure surrounded her as their bodies moved into unexpected proximity.

The fact that there was a bed right behind them didn't help either. Heat infused her face, and his hands fell from her shoulders as though burned. For a moment neither of them spoke, and she wondered if he was trying to gather his scattered wits like she was.

"I just wanted to lay down a few ground rules before . . ." He seemed unable to continue.

"Before what?" the little devil in her instinctively prompted. "Before I get too comfortable? Before I try to seduce you into marrying me for real?"

"Is that what you intend to do?"

She met his eyes, surprised at what she saw there.

Was that a challenge? He looked fearless, earnest, ready. Did he want her to try?

He looked away, clearing his throat. "I guess that brings us to rule number one. This isn't about you and me. This is about them." He pointed at the bedroom next door. "Got it?"

She nodded, still recovering from the look he had thrown at her.

"I'll be pretty busy most days anyway," he said slowly. "I've decided to start on a new album."

"Had some inspiration lately?"

"A little," he said. "It's amazing how much good material there is in betrayal."

She blushed but couldn't deny she'd deserved it. He seemed satisfied with her reaction and moved on.

"The point is, you probably won't see me most days."

Because you'll be avoiding me like the plague.

"Tomorrow will be an exception. We will have to schedule a public appearance to confirm our engagement."

That's fake *engagement to you, mister.*

"I will also call Paul's lawyers tomorrow and tell them to back off."

"You're going to call Paul's lawyers?"

"It'll be better coming from the horse's mouth."

Somehow Alexis didn't associate horses with Max's delicious-looking mouth, but his obvious protectiveness distracted her from that point for a moment.

"That's very kind of you."

He shrugged. "It's part of the deal." He paused. "Get

some sleep. Tomorrow we'll have a media circus on our hands. You'll need the rest."

Ceilia and Max usually had breakfast in the dining room at 8:30 A.M. Alexis was offered that fact by one of the staff the following morning and also extended an invitation to join them. She helped the twins wash and dress before they all headed off for their first meal of the day.

When she figured out where the dining room was, Alexis found Ceilia already sitting in there alone, sipping tea and casually looking over the paper. She rose from her chair when Alexis and the girls walked in.

"Hello, my dears," she greeted them. "Did you sleep well?"

The twins moved in close to Alexis's side, still shy of Ceilia's presence. "Yes, thank you," Alexis said for all of them.

A middle-aged woman wearing a large white apron walked in behind them. "What would you ladies like to eat?" she asked cheerfully, denoting herself as the cook.

"Yes, please let Maggie know what you want, hot or cold," Ceilia added. She looked down encouragingly at the twins. "She can make anything you want."

At that prospect, the girls seemed to lose some of their shyness. "*Anythin'*?"

Ceilia nodded. "Anything."

"Even pancakes?"

Maggie smiled. "Pancakes are my speciality."

So it was decided. As Maggie left the room, Alexis

and the twins seated themselves at the table, and Ceilia joined them.

"You know, Alexis," she said as she passed her the teapot, "I really do hope you are comfortable here, and so does Max. I know he has a rough way of showing it, but my son is a good man. He wants to do the right thing."

"I don't doubt that he is a good man, Mrs. Deroux," Alexis replied somewhat tightly. "He wouldn't be doing this if he wasn't."

"I'm glad to hear you say that. I am also glad that—" She cut herself off. "But we won't discuss that now."

Alexis poured herself some tea, trying not to be curious about what it was they weren't supposed to discuss right then. And if they were to discuss it later, when was the appropriate time?

"To be honest," Ceilia continued as though nothing had been left unsaid, "I'd like to get to know you, Alexis. I've seen you fight for yourself and your children, but I'd like to know what you're like when you're just being you."

Alexis shrugged, not really knowing what to say. "That's very flattering, Ceilia, but I'm not that complicated a person."

"What do you like to do in your spare time?"

Alexis couldn't help but chuckle. "What spare time? Ever since Kayla and Holly came into my life, there hasn't been much of that at all."

"All right, then." Ceilia nodded. "What about before they came into your life?"

"Oh, I don't know." Alexis shrugged as Maggie brought out the pancakes, much to the delight of the twins. "I love to travel. I was backpacking most of last year. I like rock climbing. I guess anything with a bit of adventure in it."

"Yes, I can believe that. What else?"

Alexis shook her head wryly. "Isn't that enough?"

"Well, I don't want you to get bored here at the house. I can't offer you rock climbing or travel. Do you read?"

"Definitely." Alexis smiled. "I've seen your library, and, believe me, you already have more than I could ask for. Besides, I'll be busy trying to get a job."

"Auntie Alex likes to take pictures," Holly announced suddenly, and both women glanced her way. She had more jam smeared around her mouth than on her pancake. As she reached for the cream, Alexis quickly beat her to it.

"Here, darling, why don't you let me do that for you?" She picked up the bowl of cream and spread some of it on Holly's pancake.

"Pictures of what?" Ceilia asked.

"Oh, it's nothing." Alexis tried to brush the topic aside. But Holly seemed to be on a roll.

"When Auntie Alex was in Paris, she took a picture of an old man, and my mummy liked it so much, she hung it on the wall at our old house."

Ceilia raised her eyebrows and looked at Alexis with new interest. "So, you're a photographer."

"No, not really," Alexis quickly denied. "It was just a

bit of fun. The old man . . . he was a peddler touting his wares on the street near the Louvre. I don't know why Mel liked it so much."

"Maybe because it was good."

Alexis blushed.

"So, have you taken any photos this year?"

"Well, I sold my camera, along with a lot of other stuff, when the twins moved in, so . . . no," Alexis explained, amazed that they had even gotten onto this subject. The last thing she had been expecting to do that week was sip tea with Ceilia Deroux and talk about her amateur photography attempts.

Just then Max walked into the room, as good-looking as ever in a collarless linen shirt and khaki shorts. Too bloody sexy.

"Good morning." He nodded at them.

On cue, Maggie walked in behind him. "The usual, sir?"

"Actually, I won't be staying for breakfast this morning," he informed her in a lowered tone. She nodded, and Alexis was irrationally annoyed at the cook for not immediately demanding why before departing.

Was it because she, Alexis Banks, was contaminating his breakfast table?

He couldn't bear to sit with her. How petty and unnecessarily insulting.

She felt her temper rising and focused on her plate to calm herself. He moved farther into the room as she talked herself out of attacking him. *I'm just being stupid. It's not as if I wanted to have breakfast with him anyway.*

Why would I?

"How is everyone?" he drawled, oblivious to her dagger eyes.

"Good!" both twins immediately intoned. He ruffled their hair as he walked past their chairs. His gaze rested briefly on Alexis.

"I just got off the phone with Geoff Rushby from Renfrey Dawson, Barristers and Solicitors."

That distracted her. "You've called the lawyers?"

Already?

"Yes, I told them that from now on I will be providing for you and the children, and you will be living with me. So you are financially secure."

"Listen, Max, about that—"

"If we're about to have another argument about whether or not I'm really going to be providing monetary assistance, let's not," he suggested. "I've already decided that I am. If you want to beat yourself up about it, do it on your own time."

"Max," Ceilia protested, "there is no need to be so harsh about it." She turned to Alexis. "But he is right, my dear. Better to let Max take care of everything for now, so at least you have a case."

"Oh, I realize the wisdom of doing that." Alexis nodded. "I just wanted to make sure he knows that, as soon as I get a job, I'm paying him back."

Max eyed the stubborn line of her chin and then shrugged. "If it makes you feel better."

Satisfied that he would take her money, Alexis moved on to her next concern. "What about my emotional state? That was point number three, wasn't it? Did they say anything about that?"

"Yes." Max grimaced. "You will need to see a psychiatrist over the next few weeks and get a medical certificate showing that you are fit and able. I'm sure you'll pass any test they throw at you."

Alexis sighed with relief. "So they're going to back off?"

"I'd say they're going to back down . . . for now," Max informed her. "But if any of the points are compromised, the court hearing is back on. We have to tread carefully. Have you read the paper yet?"

"I have." Ceilia passed down the article she had been reading when Alexis walked in. Alexis took it, and her eyes immediately fell to the photo topped by the brief headline, *Max Deroux Embraces the Family Life.*

"They're quick, aren't they?" she observed cynically.

"Which is why I've scheduled a small media conference for this afternoon," Max informed her. "So we can tell them why we're getting married."

Alexis frowned. "We can't tell them why."

"I am not suggesting we tell them anything about Paul." Max's voice was exasperated. "That would be disastrous."

"So what's the reason we're getting married, then?"

He frowned crossly. "How easily you forget."

She shrugged, trying to think what he meant.

"We're getting married," he said through clenched teeth, "because we are completely, madly, and deeply in love with each other."

"Oh, of course," she returned flatly.

His angry glare didn't abate. "I'll meet you in the library at three. Don't wear jeans, and for goodness' sake, look as if you worship the ground I walk on."

He turned to leave then, but Alexis stood up indignantly. "There's no need to get all snarky about it. You could take your own advice, you know."

He turned back. "I think the fact that I've invited three double-crossing journalists into my private space this afternoon is proof enough of my affection for you."

"Your affection," Alexis repeated disdainfully. "You're supposed to be completely, madly, and deeply in love with me."

"Well, maybe if you weren't so difficult, acting might not be such a chore."

"Children!"

Everyone in the room, including Kayla and Holly, gave the authoritative voice their full attention.

Ceilia Deroux laced her fingers together calmly behind her plate. "Be nice."

Be nice, my butt.

Max strode from the dining room. He was in no mood to be lectured by his mother, not after the morning he'd endured and the afternoon he had to look forward to. Talking with the lawyers had brought home one point to him.

Alexis was under his skin.

When he was talking to Geoff Rushby on the phone,

he hadn't been fighting for the children. He'd been fighting for Alexis. And what was he doing now? Skipping breakfast to keep an appointment with a jeweler.

Alexis needed a new engagement ring, and he was going to spend the next few hours picking one out. Did she have any idea of what that did to his sanity?

Clearly not.

She couldn't even remember that they were supposed to be acting like a couple in love. The thought, in fact, was so far from her mind that she had to be routinely reminded of it.

When he arrived at the jeweler, he had no idea what he was going to get and frankly intended to pick up the first expensive thing he saw. But involuntarily he found himself browsing, saying her name over and over again in his head like a mantra.

Alexis, Alexis, Alexis.

What he needed was something bold, brave, and beautiful.

He saw the stubborn tilt of her chin in his mind's eye.

As soon as I get a job, I'm paying you back.

She didn't take charity easily. And any fool could see how much she loved those kids, how she would do anything for them. Was she like that with everyone she loved?

And then suddenly he saw it. It wiped his thoughts and made him stop.

A sparkling gem.

A sturdy rock.

A heart of gold.

Just like the woman he'd left eating pancakes in his mother's dining room.

Alexis went to wait in the library at a quarter to three, leaving the children with Ceilia in the theater room. They seemed to be quite happy there watching *Shrek.* For the media interview, she had chosen to wear a summer dress. It was a pale blue floral print, very feminine and simply cut. While conservative, it brought out her natural curves, which she hoped Max would notice. After their run-in at breakfast, she was determined to prove to him and herself that he was attracted to her, despite the fact that he said he was "acting."

His words still stung her pride.

Sure, she had no illusions as to his deeper feelings, but there was definitely a chemistry between them that she wasn't going to let him deny.

He would eat his words.

Or get you *into more hot water than you can handle.*

She brushed aside that latent worry as the door opened and Max entered. Memories of the previous time they were in the library together . . . alone . . . bombarded her. So much had changed since then, and yet not. The sizzling awareness that had started that night had not receded.

Seduction, like smoke, weaved its cloud around her, and she breathed deeply.

He shut the door behind him, pausing with his hand still on the knob as his eyes took her in.

"Nice dress," he said finally, and advanced into the room.

He was holding something. He lifted his hand, palm up, offering it to her.

"For you."

Her knees wobbled unsteadily. "I don't understand."

He grabbed her hand and pushed the box into it. "I said I would buy you an engagement ring, and I did."

"Oh." Apprehension not unmixed with excitement enveloped her. She quickly opened the box and saw the ring snuggled deeply in the velvet folds of its casing.

She gasped.

It's perfect.

But it wasn't given in love. And for that reason she could not accept it.

"Max." She snapped the box closed. "It's too much."

"You're quite right." He nodded. "But you're going to wear it. Now hurry up and put it on. They will be here very soon."

She glanced at the clock on the wall, and time won out over pride.

Carefully she swapped the ring she was wearing for the one in the box. She had no sooner finished than the butler walked in to announce that Max's guests had arrived.

"Please take a seat." Max gestured to the sofa in front of them as three excited journalists and their cameramen were ushered into the room. The journalists sat down, and their cameramen lined up behind them, already filming.

Max and Alexis sat down on another couch facing

them. A coffee table was all that stood between the two groups. Alexis felt her nerves kick her gut, and she wanted to put a hand on her stomach to calm it. But she dared not. Would they be able to pull this off? Could Max really pretend to love her?

Seeming to sense her unease, Max slipped a hand over her bare knee, and it took all her self-control not to jump at the shock of his touch. His thumb stroked the soft skin at the base of her thigh. And suddenly the presence of the reporters faded out, as this gentle caress became the focus of her thoughts.

Somebody give me some water.

"Thank you for seeing us, Mr. Deroux," the journalist in the center of the couch began. "It's been a long time."

With effort, Alexis focused on her face. She looked greasy, like a bowl of fish and chips. Alexis knew intuitively that this woman was good for no one.

"Why the sudden change of heart?" the journalist inquired. "You haven't taken interviews in over a year."

He should have known they'd try to turn the interview to their own advantage. These slimy journalists weren't just after one story. They were after two. Curse them to hell. Why couldn't they just let Kelly rest in peace?

"I thought it was time."

He felt Alexis shift uncomfortably beside him. Was it his hand on her knee? What did she expect him to do? Just sit politely beside her? They were supposed to be in love. Or had she forgotten again?

The journalist reclaimed his attention. "Since your

exile in Paris last year, you have been adamant about avoiding all contact with the press. Why?" She smiled at him with as much warmth as a cobra.

"I think that if the press took a second to analyze its own conscience about the events leading up to my—as you put it—*exile* in Paris, they would figure it out."

"The media believe that you blame them for your sister's death, Mr. Deroux. Would you care to comment on that?"

Alexis's hand covered his, and the retort that sprang readily to his lips dissolved as her long fingers glided sensually between his. It took him a few seconds to pull his mind back to the journalist. However, it didn't matter what he had intended to say, because Alexis had decided that she was going to do the talking. Curiosity got the better of him, and he let her.

"My fiancé and I are not interested in dwelling on what essentially is old news, Ms.—" Alexis's eyes flicked to the journalist's name badge. "Jones. But if you insist, we would like some answers to a few questions."

Ms. Jones glanced at Alexis in annoyance. "I'm not sure I understand."

"Does the press intend to take responsibility for the accident that took Kelly Deroux's life?"

"No. That is, we don't consider ourselves fully to blame."

"What other parties can share the fault, Ms. Jones? Surely you are not suggesting that Kelly Deroux was partially responsible for her own death?"

"No, of course not."

"Well, if the media are at least claiming some responsibility, have they put into place any safety policies to ensure that an accident like this doesn't happen again?"

"What do you mean?"

"Well, surely if working in the field can lead to death or injury of the interviewer, interviewee, or passing bystanders, staff should be trained in safety procedures that would prevent repeat occurrences."

"Such extreme measures were not deemed necessary."

"Extreme measures! Someone was killed in a reporter's attempt to interview another person."

"And the reporter who attempted the interview was fired."

"But were others informed of his mistake? Does the media intend to abolish street chasing due to the potential dangers to its staff and the public at large?"

"I think," the journalist on the right of Ms. Jones interrupted hastily, "that this is not the story we are here for today. As Ms. Banks mentioned previously, it's all water under the bridge, and we really should concentrate on the big news at hand."

Alexis bestowed a charming smile on the man who had intervened. "What a delightful idea." Her eyes flicked to Max. "Don't you think so, darling?"

Her eyes were brimful of triumph, and he wanted to kiss her. Not because the little minx had succeeded in protecting him from these vipers but because she had jumped in without hesitation to do so. It wasn't every day that Max got rescued, let alone by a woman he'd sworn not to trust.

He was perfectly capable of taking care of himself, but this novel experience touched his heart. No one had done anything like that for him before.

But she was something else . . . Alexis Banks.

"So, the word on the street is that Alexis has moved into this house with you." The male journalist with name badge Carl Winters put forward the next question.

"That's right." Mischief prompted Max to remove his arm from Alexis' knee and sling it across her shoulders. He drew her flush against his side. She was good to hold. Warm, soft, and slender. Once again the smell of coconut and vanilla assailed his senses. Whatever shampoo she used, it was dynamite.

"As you know, Alexis and I are engaged," he continued. "I wanted her close to me."

"Could we trouble you for a few details about the lead up to the engagement?" Carl asked and didn't wait for Max's assent. "Where did you meet?"

"At a party." Max smiled down at Alexis. "We started talking, and she told me I looked as bored as a cheese platter."

Alexis's eyes widened in surprise. Satisfied that he had unsettled her, Max turned back to Carl. "She couldn't have been more right. I was bored, and she read me like a book. I guess that's what drew me to her. We were always in sync." He turned back to Alexis. "Right from the start. Isn't that right, darling?"

Alexis licked her lips uncomfortably.

"Not always," she said softly, and she looked away

from him to the journalist. "We've had our ups and downs as a couple. In fact"—her voice held the faintest hint of a challenge—"our first kiss was awkward, because I wasn't expecting it."

"I was going for the element of surprise," Max drawled to the cameras.

"Can you tell us about the proposal?" Ms. Jones asked. "When and where?"

"Couple of days ago." Alexis grinned, this time turning to him triumphantly. "I invited him over to my place, cooked him an absolutely scrumptious shepherd's pie, and he was so overcome, he proposed."

"Overcome?" Max's lips twitched. "More like stunned."

"Max, would you say that Alexis is the love of your life?" Carl asked.

"Definitely. I can't imagine being with anyone else." He was surprised by the firmness in his voice.

"And how do you feel about that, Alexis?" the third journalist piped up.

"I feel exactly the same way." The lack of doubt in her voice was equally disturbing, but he let it pass.

He lifted his wrist to cast a cursory glance at his watch. "I guess we'll have to wrap it up there. Alexis and I have some wedding planning to get on with."

"Wedding planning?" Carl sat forward eagerly. "Have you set a date?"

"Come on, Carl." Max stood up. "We can't tell you everything."

Alexis stood up too, so that it seemed awkward for the three journalists to continue sitting on the sofa looking up at them. Reluctantly, they got to their feet.

But of course, Ms. Jones had to try to squeeze out one last drop of blood.

"Before we go," she asked, "do you mind if we get a kiss for the cameras?"

As far as journalist requests went, it wasn't that unreasonable. After all, he had asked them there for *that* story. Why shouldn't they ask for the money shot? And wouldn't it prove beyond all shadow of a doubt that they were in this engagement because of mutual attraction and nothing else?

The logic was black and white.

It was just the reality that was gray. Kissing Alexis was all he wanted and all he feared. To say no would certainly arouse suspicion.

He glanced at Alexis.

She glanced at him.

They had three cameras trained on them and bunch of mood-killing journalists in the room.

How dangerous could it be?

Chapter Nine

It was sweet torture.

A gentle caress meant to haunt her.

He took her face gently between his palms, hesitated a fraction of a second as he looked deeply into her eyes, and then brought his lips down to hers. They were firm and soft, full of longing and restraint.

She trembled beneath his touch. Her knees threatened to buckle. She laid her hands on his chest to steady herself.

And then, abruptly, it was over.

He pulled away, sliding his fingers down her neck to her shoulders, seeming to center himself. "I think that's it, then."

He turned and strode out of the room, leaving her standing there with the journalists who looked as awestruck as she felt.

She schooled her expression to nonchalance with great effort to address them. "Uh . . . show's over, guys. It's time to go."

A fake smile curled Ms. Jones lips. "Are you sure you haven't got time to answer a few more questions, Ms. Banks?"

"Positive," Alexis replied, silently cursing Max for not only leaving her dazed and confused but with a bevy of salivating journalists thinking that they might be able to get more out of their meal.

As if on cue, the door opened, and Ceilia's butler walked in. "Mr. Deroux told me our guests wish to be shown out," he said.

"Yes." Alexis nodded with relief as he rounded up her reluctant companions like a sheep dog and ushered them out. The second the door closed behind them, she dropped back onto the couch, her arms flopping by her sides as she took a moment to take stock. Well, at least he hadn't completely abandoned her to the wolves. Nonetheless, his exit had been less than perfect.

I think that's it, then.

What was that?

He'd just kissed her, for goodness 'sake. Sure, it had been brief, public, and staged, but she'd felt it as potently as rocket fuel. It piqued her that he was so unaffected. That the kiss had barely finished and he was walking out the door, already preoccupied with the next thing on his plate.

Typical.

So much for proving he was attracted to her.

Suddenly she heard a phone ringing behind her. She turned around and saw a cordless on the writing desk by the window. Should she answer it? She was still walking the fine line between guest and occupant, so she didn't know whether she was overstepping her bounds. But as it continued to ring insistently, she got up and answered it.

"Sorry to interrupt, Ms. Banks, but you have call on line one. Would you like me to put it through?"

Alexis's first thought was Max, so she said yes without thinking. Of course, it was a dumb first guess. After all, why would Max be calling her when all he had to do was walk back into the room? She could have kicked herself when the caller turned out to be none other than her brother-in-law, Paul Grant.

"Do you honestly think this scam of yours is going to work?"

"Paul, I have no idea what you're talking about."

"Don't play dumb, Alexis. What do you take me for, a fool?"

"Hmm." Alexis walked leisurely back to the couch. "Do you want the honest answer or the polite platitude?"

"You think you're so clever, don't you? But this, like all your quick-fix schemes, is going to fall apart, and when it does, Lisa and I will be right there to pick up the pieces."

"You mean the children, don't you, Paul? Funny how easy it is for you to refer to them as objects."

"You know what I mean."

"I know exactly what you mean, and you can't touch me. I assume you've spoken to your lawyers."

"Of course. It seems our case is less viable at the moment, but I assured them that that was about to change."

Alexis injected as much scorn as she could into her voice. "Is that a threat?"

"No, it's a prediction. I don't know how you managed to con him, Alexis, but that engagement of yours is going to be short-lived. That brainless boy toy of yours will get sick of you, and when he does, all his money and protection is going to disappear. There's no way he'll marry you for real."

His final statement seemed to affect Alexis more than all the rest, and she sat up straight. "What makes you so sure?"

Paul's laugh was derisive. "Guys like him don't marry girls like you."

"Girls like me?" Her voice was dangerously quiet.

"You know, gold diggers with baggage," Paul snorted. "He'll have his fun, and then he'll dump you. Why don't you just save yourself the pain, and let me have the children now? What do you want with them, anyway? They would be a hindrance to your trashy Hollywood lifestyle, not to mention a disadvantage."

Alexis pulled the phone from her ear, clicked it off, and put it on the coffee table. She sat there staring at it, her fingers tingling with suppressed rage. How dare he speak to her like that!

Frustrated tears welled in her eyes. She hastily blinked

them back. The truth was, Paul's assessment of what Max thought of her wasn't really that far off the mark.

A gold digger with baggage.

It was a stigma she couldn't shake despite every attempt to do so.

She heard the click of the library door opening and hastily stood up, neatening her hair and moistening her lips. It was Ceilia who ventured tentatively into the room. The kind matriarch looked concerned.

"Are you okay, my dear? You look a little pale."

"Oh, it's nothing." Alexis indicated the phone on the table. "My brother-in-law just called. Our conversation wasn't pleasant."

Ceilia studied her carefully and then advanced into the room. "Shall I ask the staff to turn away his calls from now on?"

Alexis nodded. "That would be good." She hesitated. "Do you . . . uh . . . know where Max is?"

"Max?" Ceilia frowned. "I think he went out."

"Oh." Alexis looked at her hands. There were several other things she wanted to ask, but she dared not. Ceilia, however, was not about to let it go.

"What happened in here?" she asked. "How did the interview go?"

Alexis glanced at her quickly. "I . . . uh . . . I think it went pretty well."

"Well, that's good, isn't it?"

Alexis grimaced. *Peachy.*

"Alexis," Ceilia prompted again, "if you don't tell me what's going on, how can I help you?"

Alexis sighed. "There's nothing going on, Ceilia. At least nothing I haven't brought on myself." She tried to smile. "I have full faith that Max's plan is working. Paul was very angry at being thwarted. It's just difficult to take his insults, that's all."

Ceilia nodded understandingly. "Well, I've brought you something to take your mind off things."

For the first time, Alexis registered that Ceilia had a small black bag slung over one shoulder. She held it out to Alexis.

Alexis took the strap and ran her hands over the opening flap, and suddenly she realized what it was. "It's a camera."

"Yes." Ceilia beamed. "It's got plenty of film in it. So please enjoy yourself."

"I can't accept this."

"It's just on loan," Ceilia assured her.

For the first time that day, Alexis grinned with genuine pleasure. "Thanks."

Alexis didn't see Max for the rest of the day. The next morning, he wasn't at breakfast either. Ceilia told her somewhat apologetically that he was going to take all his meals in the music room from then on. Apparently he'd had a busload of inspiration and was ploughing through his new album. He didn't wish to be disturbed.

Alexis didn't buy it, and she could tell that Ceilia didn't either.

Max was avoiding her.

As far as he was concerned, he'd done his duty, the

children's fate was secure, and there was no further need for any interaction between them. He'd promised her as much on the day she'd arrived.

You probably won't see me most days.

She didn't know why she'd expected more. There was nothing between them but a lie. And if she had any self-respect at all, she would honor his wishes and stay out of his way. After everything he'd done, he deserved that at least. She should concentrate all her efforts on getting a job. A pity, the task was so depressing. After exhausting the possibilities of the morning's paper and having no luck at all, she decided that perhaps a little quiet fun with her new toy wasn't completely out of the question. She took the twins out into Ceilia's gorgeous gardens and took pictures of them as they played. It was a beautiful day, not a cloud in the sky, and Ceilia soon joined them with a picnic lunch by the lake. Alexis took more pictures. It was the most relaxed she'd been in a long time.

The following day, after still no word from Max, Alexis retreated to an old storeroom at the back of the house. She liked to develop her own photographs, and Ceilia had suggested she use this space as a darkroom. She didn't need to be asked twice. The paper, while holding some remotely possible job prospects, had nothing that really inspired her. She knew she shouldn't be choosy, but she couldn't help it. The other side of the coin was, she wanted a break—some time out to enjoy this brief holiday from worry.

The interview with her and Max had also just been

released. To give them some credit, the journalists hadn't said anything she didn't want them to say.

. . . So much in love . . .

. . . Match made in heaven . . .

. . . A whirlwind romance that started with a cheese board . . .

It was all quite charming. Corny, even. They even had their own tag now—*Malexis* was the abbreviation for Alexis and Max. But for a person laboring under a boulder of guilt, it was just a little too much.

Now she knew how TomKat and Brangelina felt. Of course, their relationships had one advantage over hers.

They were real.

It was only in being this close to him that she realized how much Max meant to her. In truth, she would give anything for his respect, admiration, and, yes, love.

Because, she recognized now with a shadow of pain, that's where her feelings were heading despite everything she'd tried to hold back.

Max sat at the piano, stuck in E-minor with nowhere to go. He took his hands off the keyboard and turned to look out the glass doors into a garden courtyard.

Damn it!

He reached behind him and snatched his music book off the piano. Ripping the pencil out of his mouth, he scratched out the last couple of notes he had written.

Wrong. Wrong. Wrong.

He dropped the pencil and book to the floor and went to the bar to pour himself a coffee.

Four days had passed, and it hadn't gotten easier. She plagued him like a fever. Two days ago he'd watched secretly from a distance as she'd played with the children by the lake. He'd seen the love among them. She professed to have little confidence as a mother, but she didn't need it. It came naturally. Twice he'd almost left his music and joined her. But common sense had prevailed.

She was laughing, having fun. She wasn't thinking about him at all. Out of sight, out of mind, as far as she was concerned. What would be gained by going out to her? More self-inflicted torture? More revealing of his own weakness?

The kiss in the library had knocked him for a loop. Despite its briefness, he'd never had the covers torn off his heart with such ease, and it scared the hell out of him. But at least he'd made it to the door before he did something stupid like declare himself. A long drive around town had calmed his frayed nerves, but time to think had also brought the irrevocable recognition.

He was in love with her.

It was a ludicrous deduction, considering he still didn't quite trust her. But how else could he explain his longing to protect her from everyone and everything? To take her for his own? To have her look at him the way he looked at her?

Bottom line, he was an idiot. He had no answers.

Except maybe one.

I have to stay away from her, get over this feeling.

It was as transparent as glass that his love was not

returned. He was a means to an end for her—just a way to keep her children safe. She was distant and indifferent. There was nothing left of the sexy minx in the library. That had all been an act.

Staying away was causing him a lot more pain than it was her. By the looks of things in the garden the other day, his absence barely registered on her radar. That fact only served to increase his anger at himself and decrease his writing productivity, which was never that high to begin with. He read the last two verses in his notebook with disgust.

> *Many people ask me*
> *Why are you so lonely*
> *Go and get a girl*
> *Put a smile in your world*
>
> *I know they only care*
> *And they want me to share*
> *In the joy that they feel*
> *With a love so real*
> *But you don't, babe*

He scratched out the last line. She was even showing up in his lyrics, for goodness' sake.

The day passed tediously as he struggled with his demons. He didn't see Alexis or the twins in the garden again and didn't know whether to be glad or relieved. At eight o'clock that night, he was still seated at his piano, trying to perfect the song that was no more than a page of self-pity. Who would want to listen to that? He might as well title it "Alexis Banks" and go to bed. Ripping off the page, he screwed it up into a ball and threw it at the glass doors. How could he get her out of his head?

"Hi, Max."

He turned sharply and did a double take because one of the twins was standing in her nightie right at his elbow, trying to look at the notebook that was in his lap. He hadn't even heard her come in.

"Watcha doing?"

"I'm . . ." He looked at her cute little face. "I'm . . . writing a song."

"Really?" Her eyes lit up, and a dimple appeared in each rosy cheek. "I know lots of songs."

He couldn't help but give her an answering smile. "Do you?"

"Uh-huh." She nodded vigorously. "Me and Holly can sing 'Row Your Boat' and 'Twinkle Star' and 'Baa Baa Black Sheep.' "

"That's a lot of songs." He grinned.

"Will you sing a song for me, Max?"

He had been asked just such a question by every woman he had ever dated, usually in order to establish her status among her competitors. But never had he been asked with such innocent yearning—as if he was her whole world, and if he sang her just one song, it would make her day. He had to admit, he was not oblivious to such charms. The kid tugged at his heartstrings, she and her sister always had.

"Okay."

"May I sit on the bench while you play?"

"Sure." Her lifted her up beside him. "You ready?"

Kayla scrunched up her face with delight. "Yes."

He rested his fingers on the keys and began to croon softly as he slipped into the song that had been number one on the charts for six weeks running. A gentle, soulful rhythm he hadn't sung in over year. A song he thought he'd never be strong enough to sing again.

"She gets me to laugh, when I just wanna cry. When I feel like a fool, she tells me why. Hmm, oh, yeah."

Kayla giggled, clasping her hands at her chest. "More."

He threw her a grin and continued to sing softly. "She smiles like a minx, and she sees through my soul. She knows all my faults, yet she makes me feel bold." He closed his eyes. "Hmm, oh, yeah." The memories washed over him as he was transported back to a world he thought he had left behind. "I can't see the future. I don't care about the past. But she'll always be my angel, till the very last. My sweet blue angel."

His fingers caressed the keys, flitting over them with gentle precision. He knew this song the way he knew his own heart. And he'd missed it almost as much as he missed her. He launched into the heart of the song with rough passion. "She's as wise as a wizard, quick as a clock, she has the guile of a babe, yet she knows how to shock. She's my hope. She's my faith. She's my rock." He saw her then, in his mind's eyes—sweet, young, innocent. She was smiling at him with gentle trust. A dangerous wetness began to pool at the back of his eyes.

Abruptly he pulled his hands from the keys. "My sweet blue angel."

"That was beautiful."

He stiffened sharply at the sound of another soft, lilting voice that haunted him.

What a time for her to show up.

He dabbed roughly at his eyes before turning around and saying more acidly then he intended, "What are you doing here? I thought I made myself clear about not being disturbed."

He was surprised to see tears running down her cheeks. She dashed them away with trembling hands, her beautiful brown eyes reflecting his own pain. And yet her sadness affected him even more than his own.

"I'm sorry. Kayla ran off, and I was trying to find her. I didn't want to interrupt you while you were singing."

He looked down and saw to his surprise that Kayla had curled into a ball and was sleeping soundly on the end of the piano bench.

"Looks like I put her to sleep."

"Max . . ." Alexis hesitated, and he met her eyes. "It was about your sister, wasn't it? Kelly is your blue angel, isn't she?"

He got up and went to the bar. "I really don't want to talk about it." He poured himself a drink. "Especially with you."

He could tell his words cut her, because she flinched slightly under the harshness of his remark, and immediately he felt guilty.

"Of course not. How stupid of me. I'll get Kayla and get out of your hair."

"No, wait—"

She stopped in her progress toward the bench, vulnerability in every line of her body. It took all his willpower not to reach out and pull her into his arms, beg her forgiveness for his hard words, and promise never to be so rude again.

"Don't wake Kayla just yet," he said finally. "Let her sleep for a minute." Then he lifted the percolator. "Coffee?"

She smiled gratefully.

"Yes, thanks."

They took their steaming mugs and sat outside just by the doors. Alexis allowed the peace of the evening and the smell of the roses to wash over her. For a moment they just sat there in silence, and she was content to wait. She was not going to make the first move. Not after the way he had snapped her head off just a second ago. Her skin was, after all, only so thick.

"You're right," he said, finally taking a sip from his mug. "Kelly was my blue angel."

She let out a breath she hadn't realized she'd been holding. "I really wish I could have met her."

He nodded. "You would have liked her. Everybody did."

"Were you close?"

"Very," he replied gruffly. "Even though, in the last couple of years of her life, I never got to see her much. My music career took off, and I was always traveling.

But she was my number-one supporter from the get-go. I really wish—" He broke off.

This time she said nothing. She knew what he wished. She had her own regrets when it came to her sister. Speaking about them only made them harder to get past. They both sipped from their mugs in silence for a while. She decided she had to speak.

"I love that song you wrote for her. I mean, I've heard it so many times from your CD, but to hear you sing it in person and know for the first time who it's about . . ." She pressed a hand to her chest. "I can't tell you how much it touched me."

He looked at her over the rim of his mug, his smile surprised and crooked. "Thank you."

"I'm serious."

"I know you are. I just find it funny that you've got my CD, that's all. I hadn't pegged you for a fan."

"I do admire you, Max. A lot," she added. "More than you know."

She had tried to tone down the intensity in her voice, but somehow it only seemed to come out stronger. The silence seemed to stretch forever as they contemplated each other and every unspoken feeling between them. He looked divine in the night light. Dark, sexy, and masculine. She wanted to leave her own chair and settle into his lap. Put her head under his chin, her legs over his, and his hand on her knee. He must have read something of this in her face, because he suddenly looked away.

Free of his eyes, her gaze dropped to the hand on his knee. He was clenching and unclenching his fingers.

She swallowed.

"So, what have you and the girls been doing?" he asked suddenly, maybe to distract her.

"Oh, nothing much," she sighed. "Just hanging around the house . . ." *Waiting for you to notice us.*

"Hanging around the house?" He looked up at that. "Yes, I saw you in the gardens the other day."

The fact that he'd been watching her without her knowledge made her pause. "Your . . . uh . . . mother lent me a camera. I've been taking a few pictures of the girls out there. The gardens are a great backdrop."

He nodded.

More with a need to fill the gap in conversation than anything else, she added, "Your mum really loved the pictures I took. I developed some yesterday, and she wanted to keep a couple for her albums." She drained her mug and stood up. The conversation was going nowhere. Talking to him was a strain. There was so much she wanted to say but couldn't. So what was the point?

He stood up as well, and they wandered back into the music room. He took her mug from her and set it on the counter. Their fingers brushed, and she automatically snatched her hand away.

"Have Paul's lawyers called you at all?" he asked, his voice calm, unaffected.

"No." She shook her head. "Paul did, though. I've asked the staff to turn away his calls from now on."

He looked concerned. "What did he say to you?"

"He doesn't buy it . . . among other things."

She glanced over at Kayla still sleeping soundly on the piano seat. "I should take her up to bed."

He put a hand under her chin and turned her face back to his. "What other things?"

There was no way she was going to tell him the full gist of Paul's insults. It was too degrading, too close to home. Too close to her heart.

"Nothing, really . . ."

"Define *nothing.*"

She sighed, breaking contact with his hand by stepping back slightly.

"He found it hard to believe that our engagement would result in marriage. He said you were just having fun."

There, that was close enough to the truth to satisfy him.

She put a light hand on his arm. "He was just being his usual crude self. I really should go. Thanks for the coffee."

He caught her wrist as she started to pull away and said in a voice that she had never heard before, "He thinks this is *fun*?"

Without warning, he pulled her into his arms. She stumbled between his feet, her palm to his chest as they collided. The hand on her wrist pulled her arm around his neck and held it firmly there.

"What does he know?" he rasped, clasping her face with his other hand and drawing her lips to his.

She didn't resist his onslaught. There was no time to even think about it. Nothing but raw passion assailed her senses, his and hers, blasting self-preservation to the far reaches of the universe. His lips roved roughly over hers, giving and taking with no room for choice. It was heady and rash and mind-blowing.

But above all, it was real. There was no audience. No hidden agenda. No cameras. It was just the two of them. He was kissing her because he wanted to kiss her. Not because he was trying to prove a point or perpetuate a scam.

It was need.

And the realization was an aphrodisiac like no other. Her body sang, pressing into his, wanting more.

He pulled away to look down at her. She saw the storm brewing in his eyes and knew instinctively that all she had to do was give the word and she'd be swept away.

A soft moan interrupted the moment, and they both remembered that they weren't completely alone. Alexis glanced at the piano bench.

Kayla was trembling and sweating.

"Oh, no. She's having another nightmare."

Max dropped his arms, and she went to the bench, brushing Kayla's bangs off her forehead.

"Kayla, honey, it's okay. Wake up, love. Wake up, Kayla."

"Mummy?" Kayla's eyes flew open, and they were filled with a distress no four-year-old should feel.

A lump formed in Alexis' throat as she stroked her hair. "It's okay, darling. Auntie Alex is here."

She felt Max come up behind her, so close, her bones absorbed his warmth.

"I'll carry her upstairs," he offered, and he scooped up the child with gentle ease. Alexis followed him, her eyes trained on his strong back, her outward calm belying her chaotic thoughts.

They made it to the twins' bedroom. Holly was sound asleep in one of the beds. Max tenderly laid Kayla in the other. The girl stirred again as he tucked the blankets around her, and Alexis went immediately to sit by her on the mattress.

"I miss Mummy," Kayla quavered.

"I know." Alexis lightly brushed her tears away, fighting back her own. "I miss her too. You just lie still now, and I'll stay with you until you fall back to sleep."

Kayla nodded and moved over so that Alexis could lie down beside her. "Where's Max?"

Alexis scanned the room and noted that he had gone. He must have left while she was comforting Kayla. She didn't know whether to be relieved or worried. What they had shared . . .

"Can he come sleep with us too?" Kayla interrupted her thoughts. "Maybe he can sing me another song."

"No, darling." Alexis bit her lip. It seemed she wasn't the only person Max had managed to get his hooks into today. "Max can't sleep with us."

"Why not?" Kayla wiggled up.

Alexis racked her brain for an excuse that Kayla would understand or wouldn't be hurt by. "He won't fit on the bed with us," she said finally. "He's too big."

"Oh." To her relief, Kayla seemed to accept this and snuggled her face into Alexis' chest. A few minutes later she fell asleep again, and Alexis was able to slip away to her own room.

As she slid between the cold sheets, Max's kiss came back to warm her. But so did the question, like a warning, buzzing through her head.

But what does it mean?

The next morning, Max turned up at breakfast for the first time in five days. He walked out onto the veranda with overstated indifference, wearing a pair of blue jeans and a beige V-necked T-shirt. Ignoring the three pairs of surprised eyes and the one pair of anxious ones that followed him, he went to the continental buffet on a side table prepared by Maggie earlier. He poured himself a cup of hot coffee, filled a plate with a couple of freshly baked croissants, and sauntered to the table. He sat down and reached for the jam. Alexis, the twins, and Ceilia continued to stare at him in stunned silence.

He opened the jam, set the lid on the table, and looked up at them. "What?"

"Auntie Alex told us that you were too pigheaded to have breakfast with us."

"Shh." Alexis quickly touched Holly's arm to quiet her.

Max hid a smile and spread jam on his croissant. "Well, I think I might have gotten over my pigheadedness." He glanced sideways at Alexis, who blushed rosily, and then turned back to Holly. "In fact, I'm surrendering. Waving the white flag, so to speak."

Holly screwed up her face. "You're not waving a flag."

"I am metaphorically."

Max bit loudly into his crispy croissant and met Alexis's shocked eyes. He wondered what she was thinking and wished they didn't have company. They really needed to talk . . . about last night.

"Auntie Alex." Kayla tugged on Alexis's sleeve. "What does *meta—meta—for—rickly* mean?"

Alexis didn't respond. She was too busy watching Max. And he relished it. Finally! She was as confused as he was. About bloody time. After the sleepless night he'd passed, it was good to know that she was now tasting her own medicine.

"It means"—he put down his knife and looked at his mother and then at Alexis—"that the music room is getting claustrophobic."

His mother passed a glance from him to Alexis and back again. "I see," she said shrewdly.

"What does *closs—tra—*" Kayla began again, but Ceilia hastily interrupted, addressing both twins brightly. "What do you girls think about a picnic breakfast?"

"A picnic breakfast?" Holly repeated.

"We can ask Maggie to pack us some croissants and go eat them by the lake."

The girls immediately exchanged expressions of delight. "Ooooh, Auntie Alex, may we?"

Max watched Alexis fumble. "Uh . . ."

"Your Auntie Alex is going to stay here with Max."

Ceilia took the decision out of Alexis's hands. "Cupid and Buttons are coming with us instead."

Awed, the twins turned to her in amazement. "Who are Cupid and Buttons?"

"If you come with me, I'll show you."

Their aunt forgotten, the girls immediately jumped up from their chairs and clasped each of Ceilia's proffered hands. She winked at Max before she left the room.

He had to hand it to his mother. She was master. And for once, he was grateful about it.

"Your mother," Alexis began with some exasperation, "is—"

"Exceptional," he finished for her. "I know."

He scanned her nervous expression, her wringing hands. "What's the matter, Alexis? You look worried."

"Well . . ." She paused. "After last night . . . to be honest, I'm not sure where I stand with you."

Chapter Ten

It was a bold move, jumping right to the point, but Alexis didn't see any other way to do it. Was Max after a relationship? Was he just having fun with her, as Paul had suggested? Was it a cry for help? Minutes before the kiss, they had been talking about his late sister. A shudder of humiliation disturbed the steady beat of her heart. Was he just using her for comfort?

She searched his face and waited anxiously for his reply. Why was he taking so long to say something? Was she just kidding herself about possible feelings between them?

His mouth curled cryptically, and she didn't know whether he was mocking her or himself.

"Why does any man kiss a woman?"

"Don't play games with me, Max." She stood up and

walked away from the table to the window, folding her arms protectively across her chest.

"I'm not playing games."

"Then speak plainly." The last thing she wanted was more confusion. He wasn't going to have fun at her expense, that was for sure. She might owe him, but she didn't owe him *that* much.

She felt his gaze on her back but didn't turn around. Instead, she focused on Ceilia's tranquil garden, hoping it would have a soothing effect on her churning stomach.

It didn't.

"It was a moment of weakness," he said finally. "It just happened."

Great! How flattering is that?

She swallowed. "I will not be used, Max."

"That's not what I meant."

She took a breath and spun around. "Then what did you mean?"

He put his knife down and pushed his plate away from him. "You know how attractive you are, Alexis. Do you need me to tell you as well?"

Her heart jumped at his reluctant praise. "I don't know what to say."

"It's a compliment. Take it."

She shook her head. "You were the one who made up the ground rules. You said we were living together to protect the children, not to indulge in a cheap fling."

Was it her, or did he just flinch? The movement was so small, she almost could have imagined it.

"You're absolutely right." He turned away. "I shouldn't have let it happen. I won't do so again."

The abrupt promise left her bereft. Was it possible she had been secretly hoping he would protest? He must have seen some of the discontent in her face, because he stood up and came to the window.

"Look, I'm sorry. What else can I say to make this right?"

Alexis lifted her chin, mentally gathering her dignity. The only thing she wanted him to say, she was too proud to ask for.

"There's nothing else," she sighed. "Except . . ."

"Except what?"

She considered his impassive countenance carefully. Maybe his love was out of her league, but there was really no need for all this animosity. "I really want to stop this endless bickering, Max," she began. "Can't we just be friends?"

"Friends?"

She swallowed nervously. "As strange as this might sound, Max, I like you. I admire you. I think you're a great person, and I'm grateful for everything you've done for me and the girls." She paused to let him take in her words. "Why can't we just get along?"

He sighed. "No reason at all."

"Here." She held out her hand. "Let's shake on it."

For a moment, he looked at her hand without taking it. A lump formed in her throat. He couldn't possibly mean to reject her peace offering, could he? And then, just as she was about to withdraw her hand, he took it in his.

"Okay." His fingers closed over hers with a warmth that shot right up her arm and filled her chest.

Suddenly, a burst of loud barking erupted into the room, and they both glanced at the door as two golden Labradors bounded in with the twins chasing them.

"Hey, doggies!" Kayla called. "The garden's that way!"

Alexis's laugh was forced, but she was glad for the interruption. Their conversation had reached a natural close. She had restored equilibrium. True, it wasn't the one she wanted, but it was one she needed. She threw a smile at Max to let him know that everything was okay before turning to the girls.

"Okay, ladies, round them up. We don't want paw prints all over the room."

Max watched the pandemonium around him, feeling like the eye in the storm. He just couldn't win with her, could he? He'd really thought they'd shared a special moment last night, and yet somehow it had turned into a mistake. Honestly, it was all he could do not to punch the wall in frustration. But what could he expect? He'd always known that she was indifferent to him. In fact, by her account, if anything happened between them, it would be nothing more than a "cheap fling." He had to contain his feelings. Kissing her again was out of the question. Not only had he said he wouldn't, but he'd just agreed to be friends.

Friends!

Never had he thought such a harmless concept could so greatly plague him. He repeated the word in disbelief as he watched her run after the dogs with the kids. He was a baby's breath away from taking it back. It was easier to ignore her altogether than to live with this halfway house.

He watched as Holly grabbed Cupid by the collar. "Got him!" And then Alexis seized Buttons, bending down and throwing her arms around him, a wriggling bundle of fur.

"You guys should come picnic with us," Holly suggested.

"You know, I think I will." Alexis nodded. She looked at him, simple invitation in her eyes, and his pulse quickened despite himself. "What about you, Max?"

Yep, it's official. This is going to kill me.

But he nodded anyway. "Sure. I'll be out in a second. I just need to make a couple of phone calls first."

He watched her leave the room with Holly and Cupid on her heels. A feeling of loss infused him as the point of no return cemented itself into place.

He felt a small hand slip into his and looked down to see that Kayla was still with him. She turned to him as the others disappeared out the door.

"Auntie Alex is not going to sleep with you, you know."

He almost jumped in shock at the words that sprang innocently from Kayla's lips. She tugged on his slack hand as his jaw fell open.

What the—!

"She told me," Kayla informed him, as one who carried the knowledge of the world on her little shoulders. And it appeared that she certainly did.

"She, uh . . . she *told* you that?" Max choked.

"Uh-huh."

Max knew that he was talking to a four-year-old and that he shouldn't ask. But the topic was already out there. And he couldn't help himself. He had to know why Alexis could only ever see him as a friend at best. Lifting a hand, he awkwardly scratched the back of his neck.

"Did she, uh . . . did she say why?"

Kayla cast him a look of abject pity. "You're too big."

The following week was a test in physical restraint for Max. He and Alexis got to know each other as friends. They took most meals together. They spoke about music and books. They discussed movies they'd seen. They played with the children. They joked around about past experiences. Their friendship blossomed easily, and Max's love for her only increased.

Their easy rapport seemed only to confirm everything he felt for her. It didn't help that his mother was being so coy, carting the twins off at every opportunity to get them alone together. If Alexis noticed, she didn't show it, and he didn't have the willpower to tell Ceilia that her efforts were futile.

Time spent away from Alexis was always in the music room, but he couldn't avoid her there either. Whether he liked it or not, she had become his muse, as he had first predicted. There was a song in his head that refused to be banished until it was committed to paper. The melody came first. It was bold and strong with gentle moments, a true tribute to Alexis's personality. The lyrics burst between notes as though they had always been there. Some verses were simply streams of thought he added to the music. When he was done, he felt exhausted and sated, as if he'd just gone for a long run.

The completion of the song clinched the matter for him. He realized that pride was overrated, and he had hidden from his feelings long enough. He had nothing else left to lose.

That's how he ended up outside her bedroom, clutching his new song in one hand, the other poised to knock on the door that was slightly ajar. Nerves and excitement made him hesitate. What would she think of it? Was it too soon? Should he do this "friends" thing for another week? Maybe she'd come around without confrontation.

The thing was, he couldn't wait. The CD was freshly recorded, and he ached for an opinion. It was the curse of any hardworking artist. What was the point of creativity if you couldn't share it with someone? Especially the someone who had inspired it.

It was his hesitation that caused him to eavesdrop. That had never been his intention.

"You must be Ceilia's friend. I'm sorry, you've been put through to my room by mistake." He peered inside the room to see Alexis standing by the bed, her ear to a phone. As yet, she was completely unaware that he was there.

"Oh, okay. Well, then, how can I help you?" she was saying. "Yes, those are my photos. Did she show them to you? . . . Oh . . . thank you. You're very kind to say so."

Whatever the woman was saying had clearly excited Alexis, because as she turned, he saw the huge smile on her face. He ducked back from the door frame and pressed his back to the wall.

"Really?" Alexis said. "No, I haven't heard of *Big Day*. But, yes, I'm extremely interested in working as a photographer."

Big Day.

He'd heard of them. They were a high-fashion wedding magazine . . . based in London.

His heart sank as he continued to listen.

"I think it sounds fantastic," Alexis continued. "And I really think I could do a great job for you. I'd love to be part of the project. Are you sure you don't need to see more of my work?"

There was a pause as she listened to the person on the other end of the phone and then answered another question.

"Anytime." There was a smile in her voice. "I can start anytime."

Max moved away from the door, anxious to be away before she saw him. So Alexis had accepted a job. In London, no less. It was too late.

He looked down at the CD in his hand, marveling at the futility of what he'd been about to do. She hadn't even hesitated, hadn't even paused for a breath before she'd accepted that job. Clearly he wasn't even a blip on her radar. She was going to England, and she was taking those sweet kids with her.

She didn't need him anymore. Their fake engagement was now unnecessary, and she was obviously eager to move on. He had no hold over her. He never had. Not that way, anyway. Not in the way that counted.

It was stupid to believe that in so short a time she had fallen for him as heavily as he had fallen for her. Thank goodness he hadn't said anything.

Alexis was leaving.

There was nothing left to do but get bloody used to it.

Alexis couldn't believe what she was hearing. It sounded like fun, not work. And best of all, she knew she could do a good job. A great job, in fact. She couldn't believe someone was willing to give her that chance. God bless Ceilia Deroux for showing her friend those photos of the twins; she had just unwittingly gotten her a job.

"So what do you think?" the wonderful woman on the other end of the phone asked.

"I think it sounds fantastic," Alexis admitted. "And I really think I could do a great job for you. I'd love to be part of the project."

"Then consider yourself on the team," the woman replied.

"Are you sure you don't need to see more of my work?"

"I've seen enough. You're a great photographer. When can you start?"

"Anytime," Alexis returned. "I can start anytime."

"Well, I'll get the flights organized for you."

"Flights?" Alexis repeated.

"Yes, we're based in London."

Of course. How could she have been so naive? There was a catch. There was *always* a catch.

"Alexis? Are you still there?"

"I'm sorry. I just realized that I'd be leaving Sydney." *Leaving Max.*

"Do you have a problem with that?" the woman asked.

"Not exactly."

It could be just her imagination, but she really felt as if she'd made some headway with Max in the last few days. They were really connecting. If she had just a little more time . . . This job was everything she wanted. And if she took it, she need never see Max again. And then there were the twins. How would this change affect them?

"Is there anything I can clarify?" The woman on the phone broke in to her thoughts.

"I have two children," she explained. "I would need to have comfortable accommodations near a school for them."

"That can be arranged," the woman agreed.

A few more questions later, Alexis had the full picture. It was definitely her ideal job. It had flexible hours, and it would offer her financial security and a suitable home and environment for the kids. There was no way Paul could touch her under those conditions. Intelligent thought dictated that she should take it.

Too bad she took more notice of her heart.

"I need some time to think about this."

Some time to talk to Max.

What would Max say about this when she told him? They'd gotten so much closer this week. Reality told her that he wouldn't be begging her to stay. After all, they were still just friends. Maybe he'd tell her to go for it. But what if she told him that she had feelings for him? That she loved him, that she would stay if he asked her to. Would it make a difference?

Perhaps she was expecting more than her due. If the shoe was on the other foot . . . But that didn't count. The difference was, she loved Max; she wasn't still experimenting with her feelings, the way he was.

"If you need to think about it," her potential employer was saying, "I need an answer by Friday, or I'll have to get someone else."

"I understand," Alexis replied.

"Okay," the woman continued. "Well, if you do confirm you're taking the job, we'll send you a letter detailing your salary, benefits, and the accommodations we will line up for you."

"Thanks." After taking the woman's number, Alexis said good-bye. As she hung up the phone, she knew that she had to take a chance. She'd come this far; why not go all the way?

Alexis tapped lightly on the door to the library and then poked her head into the room. Max was sitting on the couch.

"Max, could I talk to you?"

He looked at her blankly for a second and then said, "Sure."

She moved farther into the room, feeling as if she were walking into a refrigerator. The absence of warmth in Max's impassive gaze was palpable. Something had happened.

What?

She wished she had chosen a better time to raise the subject. But she was there now. It seemed foolish to leave with no good reason.

She watched as Max stuffed his hands into the pockets of his shorts and waited. "I'm all ears."

"I . . . uh . . . received a phone call today from a company called *Big Day*. They've offered me a job as a photographer."

"Congratulations," he said. "You must be very pleased. Now we don't need to continue with our agreement."

"Our agreement?" she repeated.

"The engagement," he said. "We can end it. You have financial security now. And you can move on. No doubt this job requires you to go overseas."

"I admit I am relieved that—" Alexis began, but he wouldn't let her finish.

"So am I," he agreed. "The pretense has been a strain. It will be a relief to get life back to normal and to tell your brother-in-law the game is up, won't it?"

Alexis felt a wall rising up between them as though he were laying it brick by brick. In a panic, she tried to stop him. "You're not mad at me, are you?"

"Mad at you?" He looked away, and when he turned

back, his expression was slightly less hard. "Why would I be mad at you?" He seemed to struggle for words. "I really enjoyed your time here too. I'm glad we became friends in the end. I'd really like to keep in touch with the twins if possible."

But nothing more.

She swallowed, thinking back to the kiss they had shared in the music room. The kiss that had changed her mind and broken her heart. It hadn't affected him at all.

Stupid, stupid, stupid girl. What did you expect? He's a megastar, and you're just a fly in his pie.

"Thank you." She schooled her voice to indifference. "I'm sure the girls would like that."

He inclined his head, the coldness of the gesture ripping through her heart like a blunt knife. Her fingers curled into fists behind her back.

"When will you be leaving?" he inquired politely.

Pride made her lift her chin. "As soon as possible. I will call Paul before I go, so you and your mother aren't bothered by him after I leave."

"Thanks." He shrugged. "But there's no rush for you to be out of here quickly if you'd rather take your time."

She nodded, unable to believe their conversation was ending. "Okay."

He took a step toward the door. "Well, I'll leave you to it."

Leave me to what? To put my heart back together?

"Sure."

He left the room, the click of the door echoing with finality.

She couldn't even call him a jerk. It wasn't as if he owed her anything. Reason and logic, however, didn't stop the tears from rolling quietly down her cheeks the minute he was gone. No doubt Max would forget about her and the children within a week. She looked down at the ring on her finger, and it only made her want to cry even more.

Why did I let myself fall like this? I should have known better, been more careful.

Max was not going to be an easy man to get over. This chapter of her life was going to stick with her for a long time. She moved toward the couch just vacated by Max and sat down, her face sinking into her hands. She cried till her palms filled with tears that dribbled down her wrists. But, as she always did when she hit rock bottom, she realized where she was and woke up.

If there was one thing Alexis had in leaps and bounds, it was resilience. And she knew that now was the time to muster it. Abruptly she pulled her hands from her eyes and reached across the coffee table to the tissue box sitting on one side. As she was cleaning herself up, she noticed a CD next to it. Curiosity made her sit forward. The CD caught her attention because her name was sprawled in black text over the disc.

She grabbed the CD and flipped it over to see if anything was written on the back of the protective casing. The back was white and bare. Her gaze returned to her name on the front.

Dare I?

Well, it had her name on it. Didn't she have a right to

know why? She took the CD out of its casing and walked to the back of the room to access the small stereo Ceilia used while she was reading. Turning it on, she popped the CD in and waited for the disc to read.

The gentle resonance of a piano scale pattered in her ears before Max's low, throaty voice began its sexy trill. She hadn't heard this song before. It was new and . . . beautiful. She'd never heard his voice so full of love, so full of longing, so full of hope. As she concentrated on the lyrics, the flutter in her chest began to intensify until she felt it in her throat.

Oh, my gosh. This song is about me.

The tears started to fall again. This time in joy rather than sadness. She covered her open mouth with her hands but couldn't hide the smile that broke on her face.

And then she was laughing, clutching her elbows in sheer wonderment.

What a man! What a beautiful, wonderful man. And how much she loved him. And now she knew.

He loved her too.

Max sat in the music room, alone and furious, bashing keys on the piano. Unconsciously he started playing his new song, and when he realized what he was doing, he slammed his hands on the keyboard, producing a loud, angry clang. He turned to look out the window.

There was no use thinking about what could have been. He had to put on a brave face, move on, just like her. There were good-byes to be said yet, and he couldn't snub the twins. He loved those little souls as much as their mother. Speaking of mothers, his own was going to be a problem. He knew when she realized what had happened, she'd take it upon herself to talk Alexis into staying. Somehow he had to prevent that. Alexis's heart wasn't here, and she deserved every happiness in life. He had no doubt that a stint in England doing her dream job was exactly what the doctor ordered. She'd had a rough year, and this was just what she needed. At least some good had come out of all this.

There was a brief knock at the door, and then a gentle voice said, "Hey."

His head snapped up.

"Alexis?" He turned. She had a soft glow about her as she slipped into the room. Her hair was loose about her shoulders. She looked as if she'd been crying, but there was no trace of sadness in her expression. In fact, her mouth curled with mischief, as if she were bursting with a secret. Looking at her like this was almost physically painful, so he averted his gaze. "This is not a good time."

"I won't take long. I just need to tell you one more thing."

He sighed. She was going to insist on taking her pound of flesh. "What is it?"

She came toward him, stopping just before their knees touched. She took his face between her palms. "I love you."

The words seared him.

"What?"

She smiled. "To be honest, I was hoping for a better reaction."

He stood up, clutching her arms above the elbows. "You're not . . . you're not playing with me, are you?" His voice was hoarse with emotion, but he couldn't stop himself. The feeling bursting behind his rib cage was almost overwhelming.

"Nope." She shook her head. "I love you. I love you. I love you."

"I love you too."

"I know." Her arrogance didn't bother him. Instead, it turned him on.

"You do?"

"You're the other half of me."

Realization struck him. The song. The CD. He'd accidentally left it in the library.

Thank God.

Elation assailed him. He decided to push his luck before the rush of her confession wore off. "I don't want you to go to England . . . unless you take me with you."

"What are you going to do in England?" she teased.

"Write songs about how much I love you."

She grinned. "Then who am I to hold you back?"

"Good." He returned her grin. "Glad we got that straightened out."

"Speaking of straightening people out," Alexis added thoughtfully, "*Big Day* is going to send me a letter detailing my new salary and accommodations. I think I should send Paul a copy too. You know, just to make sure he knows that he no longer has a case."

Max sighed, pulling Alexis into his arms. "Frankly,

sweetheart, your brother-in-law is the very last thing on my mind right now."

"Really?" Alexis raised mischievous eyes to his, her hands creeping up his chest. "Penny for your thoughts."

"Keep your penny," he growled, and he lowered his lips to hers. She tasted perfect, and as his hands flew into her hair, angling her face to his, he knew that this was for keeps. He was never going to let this woman go, literally or figuratively, ever again.

Epilogue

Max Deroux's Number One Single for 2009

"The Other Half of You"

Many people ask me
Why are you so lonely
Go and get a girl
Put a smile in your world
Mmmmmm

I know they only care
And they want me to share
In the joy that they feel
When love is strong and real

I don't know how to tell them that
  I've already met her

On my birthday, she'd the
Sweetest smile of allure
Until now I've been too afraid to tell
    you how I feel
The other half of me
Baby, it's you, you see

Don't worry, I know that you
Don't even have a clue
Never thought I'd find
A heart so much like mine
Mmmmmmmm, I've just been so blind

My search is done
Cause the other half of me is the
    other half of you
Baby, you're the one

I just feel like I'm living such an empty life
Nothing has any color
Everything's the same, day and night
You were one to see through my pain
Yet I'm unprepared
Cause I am too scared
To let you know I've always cared

A lot of people say
Don't let life get away
Go and get a girl

Put a smile in your world
Smile in your world

I know they only care
And they want me to share
In the joy that they feel
With a love so real
Like I have for you, babe

You're half of me
I'm half of you
My search is through
I'm just not whole
Without your soul
You fill up my heart
And that's only the start
Baby, I love you
Mmmmmm, I love you.